He had to ha...
an excellent a...

She was starting t... ...feel guilty.

Her blue eyes were suddenly huge, and she looked more like a little girl than a fully qualified doctor. 'Why were you angry with me? Because of our—relationship?' She stumbled over the words, looking bemused, and Jago's lean hands curled into fists.

'I thought I already made it clear that the past is history.'

'But it isn't, is it, Jago? It's there between us the whole time.'

'Let's just say I have a long memory for certain events.' His tone lethally smooth, he leaned back in his chair and surveyed her with the cool intent of a predator poised for the kill. It was really time for her to drop the innocent act. At least then they'd both know where they stood.

Dear Reader

I've wanted to write a book about triplets for a long time, so when my editor suggested a trilogy I knew instantly how the books would be linked. It's fascinating to observe the differences between children from the same family, and my triplets are no exception.

First we have **Katy**—she's cool and reserved on the surface, but underneath she has a wildly passionate nature that's been repressed to suit the conservative expectations of her wealthy, aristocratic family. Only one man knows the real Katy, and he's about to walk back into her life…

Then there's **Libby**—she's free-spirited and independent and has attitude by the bucket-load. It's going to take a strong man to attract her attention, and he's about to buy her in an auction…

And finally their brother **Alex.** Alex is a skilled A&E doctor, and so sinfully sexy and eligible that women can't resist him. But he isn't interested in commitment—until he meets Jenny and his well-ordered bachelor existence is turned upside down.

Two sisters and a brother from an aristocratic family, all different but linked by medicine and a powerful emotional bond, each finding love in different ways. They are the Westerling triplets, and I hope you enjoy getting to know them.

Warmly,

Sarah

THE SPANISH CONSULTANT

BY

SARAH MORGAN

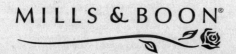

MILLS & BOON®

All the characters in this book have no existence outside the imagination of the author, and have no relation whatsoever to anyone bearing the same name or names. They are not even distantly inspired by any individual known or unknown to the author, and all the incidents are pure invention.

First published in Great Britain 2004
Harlequin Mills & Boon Limited,
Eton House, 18-24 Paradise Road, Richmond, Surrey TW9 1SR

© Sarah Morgan 2004

ISBN 0 263 83885 4

Set in Times Roman 10½ on 12 pt.
03-0304-50933

Printed and bound in Spain
by Litografía Rosés, S.A., Barcelona

CHAPTER ONE

SHE'D forgotten how much she hated coming home.

Katy's breathing quickened as she looked round the elegantly landscaped garden filled with groups of people sipping champagne and laughing together. The air smelt of summer, the heady fragrance of blooms mingling with the scent of grass mown to uniform perfection.

Suddenly she felt completely stifled and longed for the familiarity of the riverside apartment in London.

If it weren't for her mother she wouldn't be here.

'Happy birthday, Dr Westerling.'

Hearing the familiar voice behind her, Katy turned with a smile of relief, her mouth dropping open as she caught sight of her sister.

'What happened to your *hair?*'

Libby tossed her long, shaggy mane and grinned wickedly. 'I did it especially for Dad. It's called strawberry blonde. Don't you love it?'

'It's pink,' Katy said faintly, and Libby's smile widened.

'I know. It's perfect, isn't it?' Her eyes moved defiantly over the throng of conservatively dressed people and Katy bit her lip, looking at Libby's normally gorgeous blonde hair in dismay.

'Will it wash out?'

'Yep.' Libby reached out and scooped a glass of champagne from a waiter who was passing. 'But hopefully not before I've caused a spectacular firework display from our esteemed parent.'

Katy tensed, anticipating her father's anger. 'You always try and provoke him. Couldn't you have worn a slightly longer dress?'

'Definitely not.' Libby wiggled her bottom provocatively. 'Think he's going to like it?'

Katy slid her eyes over the skin-tight dress that exposed almost all of Libby's perfect legs. For a nightclub it would have been barely decent and for a summer garden party it was—

'He's going to have a heart attack.' Katy's eyes darted warily over to where their father stood, broad-shouldered and unsmiling, deep in conversation with several cabinet ministers. There was going to be trouble. She bit her lip and shook her head. 'Why do you always do this, Lib? Can't you conform just once?'

'Why would I want to?' Libby reached out a hand and touched the pearls that lay around Katy's neck. 'I've never been a pearls sort of person. And neither are you underneath.'

Katy looked away.

She didn't know who she was any more.

As usual, Libby's directness had unsettled her. 'Just because I dress appropriately for our parent's summer party, there's no need to—'

'Our *birthday* party,' Libby reminded her pointedly. 'This is supposed to be our birthday party, remember? You, me and Alex.' She glanced round the manicured garden at the hordes of elegant guests and rolled her eyes. 'We're the only triplets in the world whose parents throw them a garden party and then invite all their own guests and offset it against tax as business entertaining. Well, I, for one, refuse to play the game. And you only do it because you're so sweet and gentle and hate confrontation.'

There was a light in her eye that made Katy feel extraordinarily jumpy. 'We can all go home in a few hours,' she reminded her sister wearily. 'Just play along, Libby. For Mum's sake. Please.'

'Like you do, you mean?' Libby's eyes slid over her.

'Don't you ever want to shock them all, Katy? Rip your clothes off, get drunk, take drugs, swear?'

'All at once?' Katy gave a wan smile and glanced towards a group of men who were downing champagne at a remarkable rate.

'Ah—yes. I forgot. You can't do things like that. Lord Frederick Hamilton wouldn't approve.' Libby was silent for a moment and then she gave a sigh, her pretty face suddenly serious. 'I can't believe you're going to marry that man, Katy.'

Katy swallowed.

Sometimes she couldn't believe it either.

But it was the right thing to do.

'I mean, look at him now! Why isn't he trying to drag you into the bushes for a grope?' Libby studied him curiously, her head on one side. 'He's too busy networking to even notice that you're here. You could be naked and covered in whipped cream and he'd still be mingling with the movers and shakers.'

Everything her sister said was true and Katy wondered why she didn't mind more. She chewed her lip. The truth was that she didn't mind because she didn't *want* Freddie to take her into the bushes for a grope. She was quite happy for him to be talking to his business colleagues, leaving her alone to make her own amusement.

Freddie was safe.

At that moment their mother glanced towards them and a horrified expression crossed her face. Visibly agitated, she cast a terrified look towards her husband who was still deep in conversation and hadn't yet noticed his daughters.

Libby sucked in a breath and grinned. 'We have lift-off. Ten, nine, eight…'

The girls waited as their mother hurried towards them, Katy tense and on edge, Libby amused and defiant.

Katy glanced at her sister with a mixture of exasperation

and envy. How could she be so completely unafraid of their father?

Instead of avoiding confrontation, she relished it.

As if to prove a point, Libby tugged her dress down to expose a little more of her already exposed cleavage.

'Elizabeth.' Lady Caroline Westerling stopped in front of her daughters and her eyes darted nervously towards her husband. Fortunately he still had his back to them. 'Your hair is a disgrace, and what *do* you think you're wearing?'

'A party dress.' Libby smiled happily at her mother. 'For *my birthday party.*'

Katy winced at her less than subtle reminder that this annual event had originated as a celebration of their birthday. Her mother seemed oblivious to the dig.

'It's indecent and common.' She ran her eyes over Libby's long bare legs and winced. 'Your father will… He'll throw a fit.'

Libby's eyes gleamed. 'Oh, I do hope so,' she said softly, and their mother gave her a helpless look.

'Why, Elizabeth? Why do you have to do this?' Her eyes flickered around the lawn. 'There are any number of suitable men that you might have been introduced to this evening, but not dressed like that.'

Libby's smile widened. 'I'm only interested in unsuitable men.'

Her mother's eyes closed and sweat broke out on her brow. 'You look like a prostitute. Go upstairs and ask Sally to find you something more conservative before he sees you.'

'I like this dress and I don't care what he thinks. And neither should you.' Libby's eyes gleamed. 'You shouldn't let him bully you, Mum.'

Katy let out a breath. 'Not here, Lib, *please.*'

Libby was staring at their mother. 'You should stand up to him.'

Caroline Westerling ignored her comment and looked

away, her breathing suddenly rapid. 'Your father has some very important guests here today.' She turned to Katy and gave a bright smile that fooled no one. 'Freddie is doing *so* well. He has something to say to everyone. Your father thinks he's heading straight for the top.'

'Hopefully he'll bang his head when he gets there,' Libby drawled, and Katy hid a smile.

What would she do without her sister? She loved her irrepressible nature and the fact that no one scared her.

No one made Libby do anything she didn't want to do. Not even their father.

Katy watched Freddie weave his way through the crowd, exchanging smiles and handshakes.

Her mother gave a sigh. '*Such* a suitable man. You've made a wonderful match, Katherine. All we need to do now is to sort your job out. I hope that once you're married you'll give up all this doctor nonsense.'

Katy stiffened. 'I won't be giving it up.'

What did it take to convince her parents that this was the career she wanted?

'What about me?' Libby's tone was airy. 'I'm a nurse— does that count? And Alex is a doctor. Doesn't Dad want us to give up, too?'

Their mother bit her lip. 'You and Alex are different.'

'He can't bully us, you mean,' Libby said softly, and Caroline's eyes darted nervously around the lawn.

'Keep your voice down, Elizabeth.' Her mother looked pained and turned back to Katy. 'You've qualified now. You've shown everyone that you can do it. You don't need to carry on working any more. Freddie is extraordinarily wealthy in his own right and with your trust fund there's absolutely no need for you to work. When you're married Freddie will need you at home for entertaining clients. You won't have time for a job.'

Katy felt stifled again. 'I love being a doctor, it's what I do. There's no way I'm giving it up.'

Sometimes she felt that her job was the only thing that kept her sane.

Her mother rubbed her hands together nervously. 'You can't carry on doing nights and all those horrible hours once you're married.'

Katy liked the horrible hours. Horrible hours gave her a perfect excuse not to have a social life.

'I've got a new job starting in two weeks,' Katy reminded her. 'I'm a casualty officer in the accident and emergency department.'

And she couldn't wait.

'Oh, Katherine, what is the matter with you?' Her mother screwed up her face in horror. 'All those drunks and rough people—Saturday nights after the rugby. Why would you want to do that when you don't have to?'

Because she loved medicine. And it was a million miles away from the ruthless world of banking that had been her entire life.

The garden was closing in on her.

'It's just such a waste,' her mother was saying. 'I still tell everyone that you were a successful model when you were seventeen. You were on so many magazine covers and if you hadn't thrown it all in to become a doctor you'd be one of those supermodels now.'

'No, she wouldn't,' Libby interrupted cheerfully. 'Katy's grown hips and boobs since then and you're not allowed to have those if you're a supermodel. Just bones.'

Their mother's mouth tightened. 'Just promise me you'll give up this emergency department rubbish. I know Freddie's parents are worried about it, too. It's just not suitable, Katherine.'

Suitable. There was that word again.

Katy felt as though her head was exploding.

What was happening to her?

Normally she'd do anything to keep the peace for her

mother's sake, but today she just wanted to run screaming into the distance.

'Start the job if you must,' her mother carried on, 'but you'll be marrying Freddie in three months and you'll have to give it up then. Oh, look, there's Freddie's mother. I must talk to her about the arrangements.' She glared at Libby. 'Elizabeth, go and change into something that hides your underwear before your father sees you. *Please.*'

She turned and walked with studied elegance across the lawn, beaming at her guests and reaching for another glass of champagne.

Libby gave an exaggerated sigh. 'It's a good job we're triplets. At least they managed to get the physical contact over in one go.'

'Libby!' Katy turned to her, her blue eyes wide with reproach, and Libby shrugged.

'Well, it's true. Look at them.' She tilted her head to one side. 'They don't show each other any affection. Their marriage is a business arrangement. It's no wonder you, Alex and I are so dysfunctional. Look at our role models.'

Katy licked dry lips. 'We're not dysfunctional.'

'Yes, we are. You've spent so much of your life trying to please Dad and avoid his wrath that you don't even know who you are any more. I'm so determined to be the opposite of everything they want me to be that I've forgotten who I am, too. And as for Alex…' Libby turned and scanned the garden, looking for their brother. 'Alex is so disillusioned about marriage that he sets a three-month rule. After three months with a woman he ends the relationship just to be sure that they don't start hearing the word "serious". He's the original commitment-phobe.'

Katy looked at her. 'So are you.'

'And can you blame me?' Libby looked at her parents and shuddered dramatically. 'If that's marriage, then I hope I die single.'

'Libby, that's an awful thing to say.'

A bee hovered close to them and Libby took a step backwards.

'Oops. Killer insects.'

Katy frowned, knowing that her sister was very allergic to bee stings. 'Are you carrying adrenaline?'

Libby grinned and tapped her tiny bag. 'Lipstick and adrenaline. A girl's best friends.'

Katy knew that, despite the smile, Libby took her allergy seriously. They all did. Libby had had a frighteningly severe reaction to a sting in the past and none of them had ever forgotten it. Particularly Alex, who had been the one who'd kept his sister alive until the ambulance had arrived. Ever since then Katy had always carried adrenaline and she knew that Alex did, too. Just in case.

The bee moved away and Katy's gaze was caught by Freddie, who was taking a call on his mobile phone.

Libby's soft mouth tightened. 'Don't marry him, Katy.' Her voice was soft. 'As Mum says, there are three months to go. Plenty of time to change your mind.'

'I don't want to change my mind.'

Libby shook her head in disbelief. 'Katy, life with Lord Frederick is going to be one long round of business entertaining. He's marrying you because of Daddy.'

'I know.' Her sister's bluntness should have upset her but it didn't. It was the truth, after all. Freddie *was* marrying her because of her father's immense wealth and influence. And she didn't even care.

Libby looked at her with exasperation. 'So why are *you* marrying *him*, Katy?'

'Because I want to.'

Because their relationship was safe and predictable.

Libby shook her head. 'It isn't right, Katy. Don't you want to be in love with the man you marry?'

Katy felt her breathing quicken. *No.* No, she didn't. Love was terrifying.

Love had almost destroyed her.

'Well, maybe you can do without love, but what about passion?' Libby was studying Freddie with narrowed eyes. 'I mean, that man would never do it for me. I want someone who's so overwhelmed by lust for me that he thrusts me against the wall, lifts up my dress and takes me there and then.'

'There's nothing to lift,' came a dry male voice from behind them. 'Your dress barely covers your bottom.'

'Alex!' Libby gave a delighted squeal and threw her arms around her brother.

He glanced over her shoulder and down her back. 'Nice knickers, Lib.'

Libby grinned and tugged her dress down. 'You're late. We thought you weren't coming.'

His handsome face was inscrutable. 'I was busy.' He released her and turned to Katy, his customary indifference momentarily suspended as he looked at his other sister. 'Hi, there, kid. You all right?'

No.

Katy hugged her brother, avoiding his penetrating gaze. 'Happy birthday, Alex.'

He tucked a finger under her chin and forced her to look at him. 'All right. What's going on? Tell your big brother.'

Katy gave a wan smile. Alex had been born first by all of three minutes.

'She's being bullied into marrying Freddie,' Libby muttered darkly, 'that's what's going on. She's doing it to please Dad. It's time for the triplets to unite.'

Alex's blue eyes narrowed sharply. 'Katy?'

Katy pulled away from her brother. 'She's talking nonsense. I'm fine. Really. Just a bit tired. And nervous about the new job, I suppose.'

'A and E is great,' Alex said immediately. 'You'll love it. I just wish you'd chosen to do it further from home. You could have come and worked in my department. We need good doctors.'

Katy smiled. 'You never stay in one place for five minutes, Alex, so there's no point in joining you. I wanted to be in the same hospital as Libby and, with Freddie in the City, I need to be in London.'

'Well, of course you do,' Libby drawled. 'Which brings us back to the point I was making when you arrived, Alex. I just can't imagine Lord Frederick indulging in spontaneous sex. He probably gets his secretary to book slots in his diary. Is that really what you want, Katy?'

Suddenly Katy felt sick and she closed her eyes to blot out the images.

She didn't want sex with Freddie at all.

Alex frowned and was about to say something when their mother called him over.

'Back in a minute.' He touched Katy gently on the cheek, exchanged a meaningful glance with Libby and strolled across the lawn, lithe and athletic and totally confident.

'He's bloody good-looking. How come we're both blonde and he managed to have such dark hair? It's really spectacular with those blue eyes.' Libby watched him charm a group of her father's clients. 'He's everything a man should be. Sexy, strong, clever. The funny thing is, if he weren't his son I'm sure Dad wouldn't approve of him. He's just a little bit bad and dangerous, isn't he? And we all know what Dad thinks of dangerous men.'

Katy sucked in a breath.

She'd only ever met one dangerous man.

There was a tense silence. 'You still think about him, don't you?' Libby looked at her, her blue gaze penetrating. 'It's been eleven years since he broke your heart but you still think about him.'

Katy didn't even have to ask whom she meant. 'I—I don't…'

The sick feeling grew worse and her heart started to beat faster.

'Don't lie to me, Katy.' Libby's voice was soft. 'It all

seems such a long time ago now, doesn't it? Our eighteenth birthday party. Do you remember that summer?'

Katy stood still, her features frozen. Of course she remembered it. She remembered every single minute.

Libby's voice was soft and dreamy. 'I envied you so much. I would have done anything to have been you.'

'Stop it, Lib.' Katy closed her eyes and then opened them again quickly. Closing them just made the images worse.

'How was it that Dad used to describe him?' Libby tipped her head on one side. 'Brilliant, but dangerous. I'll never forget the first time he came to our house for one of Dad's social evenings. We were sixteen, remember? Everyone else was in a black tie and Jago Rodriguez turned up on a motorbike dressed in black leather with absolutely no respect for English social customs.'

'That's because he's Spanish,' Katy muttered, wondering why Libby was choosing this particular moment to tackle a subject that she'd studiously avoided for years.

'That probably was half the problem,' Libby agreed. 'He wasn't British and he didn't have the right pedigree. I thought Mum was going to have a heart attack. I loved the fact that he didn't give a damn what anyone thought of him. You would have thought that being the son of our housekeeper might have made him feel awkward but he had absolutely no hang-ups about who he was or where he came from.'

'That's because Mrs Rodriguez was such a great mother,' Katy said, not wanting to remember those times. 'Spaniards are renowned for having close families and she gave him pride and a belief in himself. And then Dad gave him his big break in the City—'

Libby gave a cynical laugh. 'Don't be naïve, Katy. Dad doesn't have even the thinnest streak of altruism in his make-up. Every single move he makes is calculated and he does absolutely nothing that won't benefit him.' Her tone was bitter as she surveyed her father across the lawn. He still hadn't noticed her. 'He didn't employ Jago Rodriguez out of any sense of kindness. He employed him because he spotted raw talent and the same character traits that he possesses himself. Both of them are ruthless, ambitious and completely lacking in emotional conscience.'

Katy flinched slightly at her sister's harsh analysis. It didn't match her memory of those few glorious weeks. 'Jago was kind to me, Libby, gentle.'

'He walked away without a word,' Libby pointed out grimly, and Katy sighed, unable to argue with the truth, knowing that Libby was just being protective. And she would have felt the same if positions had been reversed. Libby and Alex were her best friends and the three of them were as close as brothers and sisters could be.

And it was hardly surprising that Libby blamed Jago. The months after he'd walked away had been the worst of her life and Libby had been the one who'd seen her through it.

She bit her lip.

But hadn't he always warned her that he wasn't looking for commitment?

Had it been his fault that she'd committed the cardinal sin of falling in love with him?

'Well, he may have been a rat, but I can see why you fell for him.' Libby broke off and looked at her with a touch of awe. 'Jago was the most stunningly gorgeous male I've ever met. And to think you actually—'

'That's enough, Lib!' Katy's nails dug into her palms as memories exploded in her head.

Rapid breathing, the rough scrape of male stubble against sensitive flesh, and heat, pounding erotic heat, heat that burned inside and out...

'You—the quiet, shy one and Mr Rough, Bad and Dangerous. Where did you ever find the courage?' Libby looked at her in admiration. 'I wonder what would have

happened if Dad hadn't found out? Would it have carried on?'

*Sleek, hard muscle against soft skin, flesh scorching
flesh, mouths locked, bodies joined in untamed, wild passion…*

'Of course not.' Katy lifted a hand to her head, trying to
clear the memories. 'We were totally different.'

*His strength mixed with her gentleness. Raw male power
controlling her every movement…*

Libby pulled a face. 'That's our father talking. To him
Jago was a banned substance, right up there with drugs and
smoking. He was *the* unsuitable man. Fine for fighting dirty
in the money markets but not good enough for his daughter.
He didn't have the benefit of Lord Frederick's bloodline.'

'Maybe Dad was right. It would never have worked,'
Katy said frantically. 'Now can we change the subject,
Libby, *please*?'

*Dark eyes holding hers, possessing her, taking her with
him as their bodies exploded.*

Her sister appeared not to have heard her plea. 'Why
wouldn't it have worked? Because you were the rich heiress
and he was a bit of rough? Dad's protégé who clawed his
way up through hard work and naked ambition?' Libby
gave a wicked grin. 'I confess that I would have signed
away my share of the family fortune for the chance of one
roll in the hay with Jago. He might have been dangerous
but he was so-o-o sexy. I've always wanted to ask you
something.' She lowered her voice and glanced around to
check that no one could hear them. 'What was it like with
him? Was he good, Katy?'

Katy couldn't breathe.

Good?

Oh, yes, he was good. Better than good. Jago was so
skilled that he might have invented sex.

And she'd trained herself never to think about it. Never
to remember those few weeks. The agony was too acute.

And now, for some unfathomable reason, her sister was making her talk about it.

She never talked about it.

'That's enough, Lib.' Her voice was hoarse and she lifted a hand to loosen her collar, only to remember that her dress had a scoop neckline.

The constriction came from within.

Her memories were suffocating her.

'You loved him, Katy. He was the one,' Libby said softly. *'The one.'*

Her father in one of his terrifying rages. *It ends now, Katy. He's gone. You won't be seeing him again.*

Her childlike belief that her father was wrong.

'I kept thinking that he'd come for me,' she murmured, talking as much to herself as to Libby. 'I thought our love was strong enough to survive anything. How could I have been so wrong?'

'You were crazy about him, Katy.' Libby's tone was gentle. 'It was true love. How can you marry Freddie after what you had with Jago?'

'It's because of what I had with Jago that I'm marrying Freddie,' Katy said hoarsely. 'And Jago never loved me. How could he have loved me and walked away?'

She could see now that he'd been way out of her league. A sophisticated, ruthless man so practised in the art of seduction that someone as emotionally and physically innocent as her had never stood a chance. He'd been with her for the novelty value, whereas she'd fallen for him like a skydiver without a parachute and had been left emotionally devastated when he'd ended the relationship.

And she knew that she never wanted to experience that depth of emotional intensity again.

Which was why she was marrying Freddie.

Freddie was safe and predictable and she always knew how her body would behave around him, whereas being with Jago had been a journey into the unknown. A breathless, exciting, terrifying journey. Every look, every touch had caused an explosion inside her that had left scars.

Scars that had never healed.

'Jago wouldn't be standing around talking to your father's friends,' Libby murmured, not meeting her eyes. 'He'd be sending you hot looks and dragging you into the bushes, and he wouldn't give a damn what anyone thought.'

His voice, rough with masculine triumph. 'You're mine now, Katy.'

Desperation swamped her and she dropped her champagne glass and ran across the lawn and up the steps, ignoring Libby's attempt to stop her.

She had to get away.

Her car was parked in the front.

She'd drive.

She'd just drive, and then she'd be all right.

She could leave the memories behind.

Alex stepped up to his sister, his blue eyes narrowed. 'Did it work?'

Libby bit her lip and stared after Katy, guilt and anxiety clouding her eyes. 'Judging from her reaction, I think it might have worked a little too well. Oh, hell, Alex, are you sure we're doing the right thing? You know she hates talking about it and usually we go along with that.'

Alex rubbed a hand across the back of his neck, displaying a rare departure from his customary cool. 'She's marrying a man she doesn't love, Lib, for all the wrong reasons. Anything is worth a try.'

Libby's eyes shone a little too brightly. 'But I *hurt* her.'

'And you think she won't hurt when she finally wakes up and realises that she's made a mistake marrying Freddie? And anyway...' Alex paused and took a long slug from his glass of champagne. 'You only made her talk about stuff she thinks about all the time.'

'I felt like a total rat, not telling her about Jago,' Libby mumbled. 'What's she going to do when she finds out that he's now a doctor and working in her hospital?'

'She'll be shocked, but she needs to confront her past and get on with her life instead of bottling it up,' Alex said firmly. 'It's the right thing to do. Stop worrying.'

Libby glared at her brother. 'How come you're always so damned confident about everything? Aren't you even remotely worried he'll hurt her again?'

Alex's jaw hardened. 'We both know that Dad was somehow responsible for the first time, which was why I didn't go after Jago eleven years ago, but if he hurts her again…' There was a brief pause and the warmth of his tone dropped several degrees. 'Then I'll kill him. Now change the subject. Dad's spotted you at last and he's on his way over. Better hitch that skirt up another inch, Lib. I can't quite see your knickers.'

CHAPTER TWO

'RTA COMING in, Jago.' Charlotte, one of the A and E sisters, replaced the phone and turned to the consultant. 'Young female had to be cut out of a car. Apparently it's taken them a while to free her.'

Jago lifted night-black eyes from the X-ray he was studying, his handsome face sharply alert. 'Details?'

'Not many. Head and chest but I don't know how bad.' Charlotte tilted her head, studying his face, marvelling at how unbelievably gorgeous he was. It didn't matter how long she'd worked with him, she still stared. All the female staff stared. As one of the cheekier nurses had quipped, 'Some staffrooms have posters of heartthrobs—we have the real live thing.' Charlotte pulled herself together. 'I can hear the siren.'

Jago nodded briefly. 'Get someone to check Resus while we meet the ambulance.' With that he yanked the X-ray out of the light-box and strode through the department, broad-shouldered and confident, pausing briefly to hand the X-ray to one of the casualty officers. 'If you take a close look at this, you can see a lunar dislocation on the lateral view, Alison. You missed it.'

Aware of his reputation for zero tolerance when it came to clinical mistakes, the young doctor regarded him warily.

'I—I didn't request a lateral view.'

The consultant's voice was silky smooth. 'But fortunately I did.'

'The AP view looked normal, Mr Rodriguez—'

'Which is why you should also have requested a lateral view X-ray.' His tone was icy cold and unsympathetic and the casualty officer shifted in her seat.

21

'I—I thought that was a pretty rare injury. I read in a book that it's quite common to miss that particular injury on X-ray.'

'Not in my department,' Jago said softly, visibly unimpressed by her error. 'Next time request the right views and check them carefully. Expect the unexpected. Rare injuries still happen. Refer the patient to the orthopaedic team for a manipulation under anaesthetic and then join me in Resus. We've got an RTA coming in.'

'Yes, Mr Rodriguez.' The young female SHO was pink with mortification and Jago gritted his teeth impatiently. The girl was sloppy and over-confident and he'd be relieved when she finished her six-month stint in two weeks' time. Some people weren't cut out for emergency medicine and she was one of them. And on top of that, her longing looks were beginning to irritate him. She'd made it obvious that she'd be happy to extend their relationship beyond the confines of the hospital but he had more sense than to break hearts in his own department and these days he was becoming more and more picky about who he shared his bed with.

By his side Charlotte winced. 'Ouch—you were hard on her.'

Jago lifted a dark eyebrow, his expression cool. 'You'd prefer that she discharged a patient with a dislocation?'

'No, but—'

'Patients have the right to expect the very best care when they come into this department. She has a great deal to learn.'

Ending the conversation abruptly, Jago pushed his way through the swing doors just as the ambulance roared into the ambulance bay.

The paramedics opened the back and lifted out the stretcher. 'Young female with head and chest injuries. She was shunted from behind so we've had her on a backboard. GCS of 7 at the scene but she regained consciousness fairly quickly and it's 12 now, but she's not saying much.' The paramedic frowned. 'She hasn't been able to tell us her name or anything, but we've got her bag so we need to try and find out who she is.'

Jago turned to look at the still form of the girl lying on the trolley and his powerful body froze in shock. He stared in stunned disbelief, his muscular shoulders tense as his eyes raked over the blonde hair and the endless limbs.

I love you, Jago.

'I know who she is.'

Only years of exercising rigid control over his intrinsically volatile emotions prevented him from displaying his reaction to her in a very public way.

The paramedic was looking at him. 'You do? Oh—right. Well, in that case...'

'Take her through to Resus,' Jago ordered, his eyes still on the long, primrose blonde hair, now matted with blood.

Do you think I'm pretty, Jago?

'Her air bag didn't open properly and she hit the windscreen,' the paramedic explained as they manoeuvred the stretcher into the A and E department. 'Her head bled a lot and she's going to need stitches, but we've put a pad on it for now. She might have chest injuries, too, from the way she was thrown against the steering-wheel. Weird really. There didn't seem to be anyone else involved. You should have seen the car. Frankly, she was bloody lucky to escape alive.'

Jago's expression didn't flicker, his eyes as black as night and his manner controlled and totally professional. 'OK, guys, let's get to work. Get me some gloves, please—she's covered in glass. Be careful!'

Someone handed him some gloves and he pulled them on quickly as Charlotte moved closer to the trolley.

'Hello, can you hear me, er...?' She glanced up questioningly. 'Do we have a name?'

'Her name is Katherine.' Jago checked her airway and reached for an oxygen mask. 'Katherine Westerling.'

Huge blue eyes staring into his, innocence mingling with excitement and anticipation as his hard body moved against her softness...

'Right.' Charlotte exchanged puzzled glances with one of her colleagues. 'Why is that name familiar?'

'She's the daughter of Sir Charles Westerling, the banker,' Jago informed her tautly, and Charlotte's eyes widened.

'Wow! I've seen pictures of her in the glossies, looking glamorous. She's seriously rich and really, really beautiful.'

And totally lacking in morals.

His relationship with Katy had been the one and only time in his life that he'd lowered his guard with a woman. And he hadn't made the same mistake since.

Her father, telling him the truth, showing him the evidence...

'That's her.' His emotions held rigidly in check, Jago didn't look up, his hands moving swiftly as he worked to stabilise Katy. *She was just a patient.* 'Now, can we stop gossiping and just get on with the job?'

Charlotte stiffened warily, cast him a curious look and then turned her attention back to the patient. 'Katherine? Katherine, can you hear me?'

Katy lay with her eyes closed.

She could hear voices but she didn't respond. It felt nice to hide in the darkness. There was a sharp prick in her arm and hands moving over her.

'Katherine.'

A kind female voice was calling her name but it felt like too much effort to respond.

Then she heard a harsh, male voice and her body tensed. It sounded so familiar.

'Her X-rays are fine but she's got a laceration by her

hairline that's going to need suturing and she was knocked out so she's going to have to stay in overnight for observation.' Fingers touched her and then she heard the voice again. 'She's shivering. Get some blankets.'

Something soft and cosy covered her immediately but the shivering wouldn't stop.

'Any relatives?'

'She was on her own in the car.'

'Open your eyes, Katherine.'

Hands touching her, the prick of another needle.

'OK, she's stable.' The familiar male voice again. 'I'll leave you to get on with it. Get her a bed on the ward and call me if anything changes.'

'How's that head?'

Katy lay in the bed, watching the nurse who was checking her blood pressure. 'Aching, but I'll live.' She moved her head to look around her and then winced as pain lanced through her skull. 'Which hospital am I in?'

'St Andrew's. We put seven stitches in your head but your hair will cover it so don't worry about having a scar.'

St Andrew's?

Katy closed her eyes and suppressed a groan. Having a scar was the least of her problems. She was due to start work in this very department in two weeks' time. How embarrassing!

Should she say something?

Deciding to remain silent on the subject for the time being, she shrank lower in the bed.

'They reckon you're lucky to be alive.' The nurse pulled a pen out of her pocket and scribbled on the chart. 'What happened?'

'I don't know.' Katy frowned as she tried to remember. 'I was at a party at my parents' house and then I left to drive home.' *Running from her past.* 'I saw a rabbit in the road so I slammed on my brakes and that's the last thing I remember.'

The nurse made a clucking sound. 'Anyway, your X-rays are clear so you should be able to go home in the morning. We found some details in your handbag and called your fiancé. He's on his way over.'

Katy suppressed a groan. She didn't want to see Freddie. Why couldn't they have called Libby or Alex?

The nurse was looking at her in concern. 'You look terrible. Is there anything I can get you? Do you need anything?'

Yes. She needed to know that the voice that she'd heard in A and E hadn't been Jago's.

Of course it wasn't Jago's, she told herself.

Jago was a super-rich banker. How could he possibly be working in A and E?

She had just been imagining things and it was no wonder after the conversation she'd had with Libby.

'I don't need anything else, thanks.'

She smiled at the nurse just as the door opened and Jago Rodriguez walked in.

The colour drained out of Katy's cheeks and her breathing did an emergency stop. Her entire body was frozen to the bed, paralysed by the shocking reality of being confronted by Jago.

'Mr Rodriguez.' The nurse straightened nervously, went a deep shade of pink and dropped the chart she was holding.

Stunning dark eyes flickered to the nurse. 'You can go.'

He held the door open in the manner of someone totally accustomed to having his every instruction obeyed instantly, and the flustered nurse retrieved the chart and hurried across the room, casting a final hungry look at Jago's profile before slipping outside.

Suddenly the room seemed too small.

Jago closed the door and stood with his back to it, his

long, powerful legs spread apart, his expression unsmiling. Dominant, confident and unapologetically male, not by the slightest flicker of those sinfully dark lashes did he acknowledge that they'd ever been more than casual acquaintances.

'Hello, princess.' He spoke in a deep, masculine drawl that made Katy's pulse race. 'Running again?'

Katy's soft lips parted and she struggled to sit up. She was in total shock. The subject of all her dreams and nightmares was suddenly confronting her. Jago, whom she'd thought about every waking minute for the last eleven years.

Jago, whom she'd never expected to see again.

Somehow he was standing in her hospital room, frighteningly imposing and super-handsome, displaying not the slightest discomfort at seeing her. Nothing in his body language suggested that he felt the smallest hint of guilt or remorse for the way he'd walked away from her without a word of explanation, leaving her so badly hurt that for a while she'd thought she'd never recover.

She could see that he was waiting for her to speak but she was totally unable to think coherently.

Over time she'd managed to convince herself that her starry-eyed view of him had been coloured by a hormonally driven teenage imagination. She'd decided that he couldn't have been as gorgeous as she remembered.

She'd been wrong.

Jago Rodriguez was strikingly good-looking. He wore his glossy dark hair so short that in any other man it would have accentuated the faults in his facial features. But Jago didn't have any faults. He possessed a bone structure that made artists drool and a physique that would have driven athletes to a state of mindless envy. He was impossibly, staggeringly handsome.

And to set him apart from the average man still further,

he wore an exquisitely tailored suit that skimmed his wide shoulders and just shrieked of designer label.

In a strange moment of distraction Katy found herself wondering what happened if a patient was sick on it.

Growing hotter and hotter under his steady scrutiny, she lifted a hand to her aching head.

'Wh-what are you—?' She broke off, totally unable to believe his presence by her hospital bed. 'I-I didn't know you were a doctor,' she croaked, and a dark eyebrow swept upwards.

'Why should you?'

Why indeed?

After all, he'd chosen to walk out of her life without a backward glance or giving a forwarding address. To him the relationship had been over and he'd moved on. Unfortunately it hadn't been so easy for her.

She dug her nails in her palms. 'I assumed you were still in banking.'

'I lost my taste for banking,' he said smoothly, his dark eyes fixed on her pale face. 'I changed career.'

So that was why her feeble, childish attempts to track him down had failed. She'd used all her contacts at the various banks but with no success. It had never occurred to her that he might have changed profession.

Katy blinked as she did the calculation in her head. If he was a consultant now then he must have started training immediately after he'd left her father's company and he must have progressed fast. But, then, that didn't surprise her. Jago had always been frighteningly clever.

'Why medicine?'

And why this hospital, where she was going to see him every day?

She fought the rush of panic that threatened to swamp her and focused on his tie. Silk. Designer. Sufficiently muted not to induce a headache in a patient with a head injury.

'I like the adrenaline rush. When you're dealing with lives, the stakes are higher than in the money markets.'

He gave a careless shrug and she found her gaze drifting upwards to his powerful shoulders. If anything, he was even more spectacular than he'd been eleven years before. Jago Rodriguez was sex in the raw, so overwhelmingly masculine that just looking at him was enough to punch the breath from her body.

Appalled by her own thoughts and the traitorous stab of awareness that she felt low in her stomach, she looked away from him.

What was the matter with her? He'd been in the room for less than five minutes and already her insides were turning somersaults. Did she have absolutely no sense of self-preservation?

It depressed her that she could still react to him, knowing just how badly he'd hurt her. Weren't doctors supposed to be warm and caring?

For a short, blissful interlude she'd thought that Jago possessed those qualities, but experience had shown that he was capable of being every bit as ruthless, ambitious and macho as her father.

Jago didn't have a compassionate bone in his body and she certainly couldn't imagine him as a doctor.

As far as she was concerned, he wasn't doctor material.

She started to shiver.

Why now? Why did she have to bump into Jago now, when she'd finally managed to rebuild an emotionally comfortable life for herself?

She was marrying Freddie and she was never again going to feel that breathless, stomach-churning excitement that she'd experienced with Jago.

Those slumberous eyes, as dark as obsidian, reflected not a hint of warmth or tenderness. Nothing that reflected the intense emotions which had characterised their relationship. The tension in the room sucked the breath from her body but he surveyed her with an almost indifferent coolness that made it blatantly clear he had no positive feelings for her whatsoever.

It was almost as if the very sight of her offended him, which was utterly ridiculous. After all, *he'd* been the one who'd walked away from *her* without the smallest explanation.

And maybe that shouldn't have come as such a surprise. She'd been well aware of his reputation when she'd become involved with him. In fact, his reputation had been part of the fascination, at least to begin with, and he'd always warned her that he didn't do commitment.

So why had she been so devastated when he'd ended it? And did she really expect him to be harbouring romantic memories about her? Just remembering all her innocent fantasies about him filled her with mortification.

She'd been so naïve.

She suddenly felt horribly vulnerable in her NHS nightie that was open all the way down the back.

If she had to face Jago she would have chosen to be wearing armour.

'I heard your voice when the paramedics brought me in.' Her voice was a croak. 'Was it you who—?'

'Who sorted you out? Yes, it was. I seem to make a habit of it, don't I? And it's always on the same date.' He strolled forward and sat on the edge of the bed. 'Tell me, Katy. What were you running from this time?'

'Nothing.'

Her memories.

'You could have been killed. It took them an hour to cut you out of the car.' His tone was matter-of-fact. 'Do you think I've forgotten the significance of today, Katy? It's the tenth of July. Your birthday. So the question is, what are those unspeakable parents of yours trying to force you to do this time?'

Their eyes clashed and she knew that he was remembering her eighteenth birthday eleven years previously. Another occasion when she'd been running and he'd rescued her...

'I'm going to be a doctor.'

Katy faced her father, her heart beating so fast that she felt faint. There wasn't going to be a row. There couldn't be. They were surrounded by influential people. She'd chosen to confront him in the middle of their birthday party, knowing that he wouldn't be able to do much.

Her father looked at her impatiently. 'Don't be ridiculous, Katherine. You're going to do this cordon bleu cookery course in Switzerland. I've paid the fees.'

Katy took several gulps of air and realised that her father was so dismissive of her that he didn't even listen to her any more.

'But I don't want to cook, and I don't want to model,' she said hesitantly, refusing to let the subject drop, digging her fingers into her damp palms as she faced her father. 'I'm going to be a doctor.'

She'd applied for a place and had been accepted subject to her exam results. Telling her father was the last step to achieving her dream.

Her father's expression became ugly, his stance suddenly menacing. 'You're not. It's bad enough that Alex has chosen to be a doctor when he's got the brains to join me and make a fortune in the City, without you doing the same thing.'

Katy refrained from telling him that it had been glancing through Alex's prospectuses from medical school that had helped her finally make up her mind. She'd already wasted enough time modelling.

Now she was going to study medicine.

'You have the looks to be a highly successful model,' her mother added nervously, lifting a hand to wave at one of the guests and pinning a false smile on her face. 'Thanks to your father, you're wealthy enough not to have to work. Have some fun until you meet someone suitable and then get married.'

'But I want to work,' Katy blurted out, forgetting that they were surrounded by people. 'I want to earn a living. *I want a career.*'

'Lower your voice, Katherine!' Her mother's tone was a soft mutter and she glanced round self-consciously. 'Your father has important guests here. We don't want everyone gossiping.'

Katy gritted her teeth. She didn't care about gossip. She just wanted him to listen to her for once. For once she wanted him to respect her opinion on something.

'Please Dad, I—'

'The subject is closed, Katherine.' Her father's face was cold and unsmiling. 'On the first of October you're going off to your cookery course and that's the end of it. Don't mention it again or you'll make me angry.'

And Katy knew exactly what that meant.

Her heart started to beat faster and she dug her nails deeper into her palms. It was the threat of her father's fury that had prevented her from saying something before now. She'd sneaked off to interviews, accepted Alex's help in finding accommodation and the only thing left to do now was to tell her parents.

And she was going to tell them.

'Dad—'

'I don't want the subject mentioned again.' With that her father strode off across the lawn to talk to the guests, leaving Katy with a desire to scream with frustration.

How was she ever going to get her father to accept her plans?

Suddenly it was all too much.

Tears springing into her eyes, she spun round and ran across the lawn, ignoring the astonished looks she received from the guests, ignoring her mother's frosty glare.

She didn't slow her pace until she reached the stables. There was only one thing that would ease her tension and that was a ride. She needed to get away from her own party.

Brushing the tears from her cheeks, she grabbed a bridle from the tack room, relieved that the grooms were obviously busy elsewhere. Then she hurried back across the yard and slid into one of the stables.

'Hi, sweetheart.' She stroked her favourite mare on the neck and slipped the reins over the horse's head and the bit into her mouth, fastening the bridle quickly. 'We're getting out of here.'

She led the mare out into the yard, slipped off her high heels and vaulted easily onto the horse's back, clattering out of the yard before anyone spotted her.

The moment she reached the fields she kicked the horse into a gallop and sped along the track at a breakneck pace.

Part of her knew it wasn't safe. She was wearing a loose summer dress and no riding hat and she was crying so hard she couldn't see where she was going, but she just *had* to get away.

She headed for the barn at the far end of her father's estate. The place she always escaped to when she didn't want anyone to find her.

As she approached the barn the horse suddenly veered to the left to avoid a ditch. Katy lost her balance and slid off the animal's back, landing awkwardly in the long grass.

She lay still for a moment, staring at the sky, wondering which part of her she'd hurt most.

'Well, that was dramatic.' The low masculine drawl came from beside her and she struggled to sit up, her eyes widening as she recognised the man staring down at her.

Jago Rodriguez.

He worked for her father in the bank and everyone knew who he was. *Especially the women.* He'd clawed his way up from what could only be described as an underprivileged background. But if nature had deprived him of material wealth, it had more than compensated by giving Jago sensational good looks, a ruthless ambition to succeed and a brain as sharp as the business end of a razor. It was those qualities that had brought him to the attention of her father and had made him a millionaire several times over by the time he was in his early twenties.

He was a frequent visitor to the manor and Libby often sat on the stairs, hoping for a glimpse of him. Katy wasn't so bold. She hid in the shadows and watched in mute admiration as Jago coolly ignored her father's moodiness and childish displays of temper. He was one of the few people who remained completely undisturbed by Charles Westerling's thoroughly abrasive business manner and bully-boy tactics.

'The boy's brilliant,' her father would grunt as they ate dinner in the formal dining room after Jago had left. Of course, he was never invited to join them. 'Has an instinctive feel for what will work and goes with it. He's making a fortune for himself and the bank at the moment.'

Their mother looked pained. 'I just wish you didn't have to invite him to events here. He has absolutely no respect for English social convention.'

'Hallelujah,' Libby muttered, and Katy stared at her plate, wishing that she had just one small portion of Jago Rodriguez's courage.

What must it be like to have such self-confidence that you didn't care what people thought?

'I think he's gorgeous,' Libby piped up, and then subsided as she met her father's glare.

'I know he's got a dreadful reputation with women, but I bet he's a brilliant kisser,' Libby said later as they got ready for bed, both of them lost in their own fantasies about Jago. 'I wonder if he'd kiss me just once so that I could find out what it feels like to do it properly.'

Lying in a tumbled heap and staring into his wicked,

masculine face, Katy remembered her sister's comment and felt her heart miss a beat.

'What are you doing here?'

'Escaping,' he said dryly, glancing in the direction of the manor house where the party was still in full swing. 'Just as you are, presumably.'

He was expecting an answer but suddenly she found herself horribly tongue-tied and totally unable to speak.

He hunkered down next to her, lifting a dark eyebrow as she shrank away from him. 'Ah—the shy sister who always avoids me. You know, you shouldn't believe everything you hear.' He sounded mildly amused. 'I don't seduce children.'

She blushed hotly, mortified that he'd read her mind and self-conscious about her appearance. 'I'm not a child.' She brushed her tangled blonde hair away from her face and looked at him shyly. 'It's my eighteenth birthday today.'

She was supposed to be a woman.

'I know that. I was invited to the party. If party is the right word.' His voice was soft and his gaze assessing as it slid over her body with a thoroughness that left her gasping for air. 'So why are you galloping across the fields wearing a party dress and not much else? Why aren't you mingling with your guests?'

'They're mostly my parents' friends and colleagues. Contacts.' She stared into those lazy dark eyes and fought the temptation to blurt out all her problems. What was the point? A man like Jago wouldn't begin to understand what it was like to have someone dictating your life. He never let anyone dictate to him. 'I needed to get away.'

'Hardly surprising. If someone gave me an eighteenth birthday party like that I'd want to get away, too.' His gaze moved down her bare legs and rested on her feet. 'What happened to your shoes, Cinderella?'

'I left them at the stable.' She tried to scramble to her

feet and then gave a yelp of pain as her ankle gave way. 'Ouch!'

Tears pricked her eyes and she blinked them away, determined not to cry in front of him.

He frowned sharply. 'Let me look at that.'

Without waiting for her permission he slid a strong hand down her leg and examined her ankle. She held her breath and stared in fascination at his long, strong fingers as they moved over the bone, pressing and testing her reaction. Finally he straightened. 'It's not broken. You must have sprained it when you fell. You're lucky you didn't fracture your skull.'

Strands of her blonde hair trailed onto his forearm and she marvelled at the contrast between them. He was so dark and strong and everything about him was so different to her. Hypnotised by his masculinity, her eyes fixed on the dark hairs on his forearms, travelled slowly upwards over the swell of muscle and then lifted to the stubble shadowing his hard jaw. He was breathtakingly gorgeous and so sexy that her imagination took flight.

She felt a flutter in the pit of her stomach and her eyes dropped to his firm mouth, wondering, *wishing* …

He met her rapt expression with a lazy amusement that was totally male. 'Stop looking at me like that, princess, or I just might do what you want me to do.'

She blushed and sank her teeth into her lower lip. Miles from anywhere, frustrated beyond belief with her life, she felt suddenly bold. 'I want you to kiss me.'

She stood totally still, shocked by her own impulsive declaration, but his expression didn't flicker.

'I know you do.'

His wicked dark eyes slid down to her mouth and suddenly her breathing was choppy.

'So will you?'

His gaze lifted. 'No.'

Her fragile bubble of confidence exploded and she stumbled to her feet, wincing at the pain in her ankle. 'Because you're scared of my father?'

He threw back his head and laughed. A rich, masculine sound that made her toes curl.

'What do you think?' He was still smiling and she swallowed.

'I don't think you're scared of anything.' She stared down at her feet, mortified by his rejection. 'So it's because I'm not pretty enough.'

There was a long, electric silence and then he slid strong fingers under her chin and forced her to look at him.

'You're beautiful, princess, and you know it.' His voice was soft and he moved his hand and ran his fingers through her blonde hair with the same easy confidence that he applied to everything. 'So beautiful that it hurts to look at you.'

'So why won't you kiss me?'

'Because I'm too old to sneak around kissing children.'

'I'm not a child!'

One dark eyebrow lifted. 'So why were you running away? Grown-ups don't run away from problems, Katy. They face them. When you've got the courage to kiss me in full view of your father, come back and we'll talk.'

Grown-ups don't run away from problems.

And here she was, running again…

She stared at Jago, thinking that he hadn't changed much. He might be a doctor but it certainly hadn't softened him. He looked tough and uncompromising and totally self-assured. But, then, Jago Rodriguez had always had confidence by the bucketload.

Ironic really, she reflected as she tightened her fists on the sheet. For all her privileged upbringing she'd never managed to achieve much in the way of confidence.

'I'm still waiting for you to tell me what you were running from.'

There was a tap on the door and the nurse opened it warily.

'Miss Westerling's fiancé is here.'

Jago's eyes lifted to Katy's.

There was a long, aching silence and then he stood up, his eyes shuttered. 'Show him in.'

Freddie came striding in, hidden behind a bouquet of flowers the size of Africa. Despite the pain in her head, Katy gave a weak smile. Unlike Jago, Freddie never veered from protocol. He couldn't possibly visit someone in hospital and not take flowers.

Freddie presented the flowers and leaned over to kiss her awkwardly on the cheek. 'Katherine! What the devil happened?'

Katy was hopelessly aware of Jago's dark scrutiny. 'I— I crashed my car.'

Freddie looked perplexed. 'None of us even knew you'd left the party.'

'Nothing changes,' Jago murmured in an undertone, but only Katy understood the implications of his softly spoken words.

'Are you the doctor who sorted her out?' Freddie extended a hand, his cultured drawl the product of an exclusive public school education. 'Can't thank you enough. Will she be all right?'

'She was lucky. The damage was superficial,' Jago said, his eyes drifting to the dressing on Katy's forehead. 'Stitches out in seven days and the scar will be under the hairline. She'll be modelling again in a few weeks without a mark to show for it.'

Freddie frowned and Katy realised that Jago didn't even know she was a doctor. Especially not a doctor who was going to be working for him in this department in two weeks' time.

Or would she?

Could she really take a job alongside the one man who had the ability to dishevel her otherwise ordered life?

She couldn't believe that fate would do this to her.

On the other hand, working in A and E was what she really wanted, and if she gave up her father would think he'd won and she'd lose the career she loved.

She looked at Jago. For eleven years he'd been haunting her life. In the shadows of everything she did.

Maybe the only way she was going to move on was to face up to the past.

He was just a man after all.

A man who obviously hadn't loved her. *A man who wasn't capable of loving anyone.*

She had more sense than to fall for Jago again.

And she was marrying Freddie.

Conservative, British Freddie who respected convention, could trace his family back six hundred years, spoke with the right accent and always tried to do the right thing.

'How long does she need to stay in?' Freddie glanced discreetly at his watch and Katy almost laughed. He was so transparent. He obviously had a meeting that he was desperate to get to. It was like her father all over again. Only Freddie was much, much nicer than her father.

'You don't need to stay, Freddie,' she said gently, and Freddie gave an awkward smile.

'It's just that I've got dinner with one of the managing directors from Fixed Income and—'

'It's OK.' Her head was throbbing too much to hear about banks. 'I'll be fine. I'll be going home tomorrow. Libby can fetch me. I'll call you.'

'Well, don't worry about the car.' His mind clearly on other things, Freddie leaned forward and gave her another awkward kiss on the cheek. 'I'll buy you a new one as a wedding present.'

Katy's eyes slid to Jago but his face gave nothing away, his thick, dark lashes concealing the expression in his eyes.

She remembered her father saying that it had been his in-scrutability and cool head that had made him such a fear-some reputation at such a young age.

'I'll be in touch, then.' Freddie slid out of the door, leaving the two of them alone once more.

'So he's the reason you were running.' Jago's voice was even and suddenly Katy felt exhausted.

She just wanted to close her eyes and sleep for ever. She wished her head would stop throbbing.

'Go away, Jago.' *Before she made a total fool of herself in front of him.*

'Your father's choice, I presume. I can't believe you're marrying him,' he drawled softly. 'He's totally wrong for you.'

Weakened by her injury and the shock of seeing him again, Katy roused herself sufficiently to defend herself.

'He's totally right for me. I *want* to marry Freddie.'

'Do you? So, tell me, Katy…' He leaned forward, his voice suddenly soft. 'If it's what you want, why did you just drive your car into a ditch?'

CHAPTER THREE

JAGO strode back to his office, tense and on edge, shaken out of his customary cool by his encounter with Katy.

Why the hell had he gone and seen her personally?

He could have arranged for a more junior doctor to check on her and discharge her, but instead he hadn't been able to resist seeing her one more time.

Some self-satisfied, macho corner of his make-up had wanted to see her awake, to test her reaction to him.

He'd walked away eleven years before, too angry to risk seeing her face to face. Confronted by her after all this time, he'd suddenly wanted to see if there was even the slightest hint of guilt or discomfort in that beautiful face.

There hadn't been.

Oh, she'd been shocked to see him, but she'd met his gaze steadily, without the slightest hint of remorse. A man with less experience than him might have thought she was as innocent as the day she was born, but he knew better.

Katy's innocence was only on the surface.

He opened the door to his office, anger erupting inside him at the memories her presence had reawakened. Until he'd met Katy, he'd always prided himself in his lack of vulnerability when it had come to the female sex. He'd been streetwise and sharp and able to recognise every one of their tricks.

He shouldered the door shut behind him and swore softly in Spanish. Katy was the only woman in his life who'd managed to sneak under his defences. Her fragile innocence and femininity had appealed to everything male in him and he had been totally unprepared for the strength of his reaction to her. She had been so far removed from the type of woman he'd usually spent time with that to begin with he'd avoided her, but her blatant fascination in him had proved impossible to resist.

He tried to ignore her lush curves and told himself that his taste didn't run to innocent schoolgirls, however beautiful. *And Katy was astonishingly beautiful.* An incredible heart-shaped face surrounded by a cloud of silken blonde hair that could make a man lose his mind. At eighteen she possessed a sweetness that had stifled his usually measured reaction to the opposite sex.

There was something about those huge blue eyes, about the way she watched him with a mixture of excitement and longing, that gradually eroded his already severely tested self-control. Given the temptation, maybe it wasn't so surprising that he behaved like a hormonal teenager, allowing the power of sexual attraction to overwhelm common sense.

It amused him to take her out and watch the havoc that her presence caused. She was so dazzling that wherever they went she attracted the maximum amount of male attention, attention that went completely unnoticed by Katy herself because she was never able to drag her eyes away from *him*.

And her blatant and naïve adoration of him was both a source of amusement and smug male satisfaction.

She was his and only his.

Knowing her to be sexually inexperienced, for the first time in his life he was forced to curb his own physical needs until he judged that she was ready. And when that moment came, he derived an astonishing measure of gratification from peeling away the layers of shyness and reserve to reveal the hot, sexual nature that he'd detected from the first time he'd seen her.

He gritted his teeth as he remembered just how passionate a nature his patience had revealed.

Too passionate.

When her father took him to one side and told him the truth about her, he was stunned by the depth of his own disappointment and distaste.

Stunned by the emptiness he felt, he walked away in a state of shock and never contacted her again, grimly aware that he'd let her touch him in ways that weren't exclusively physical.

I love you, Jago.

He tensed, reminding himself of the truth. That her declarations had proved as shallow and fragile as her promises of commitment.

And now she was engaged to be married.

Freddie was so obviously the suitable man.

And Katy would make an excellent businessman's wife.

Jago stared fixedly out of the window, wondering why he wanted to put a fist through it.

'Did you slap his face?' Libby curled up on Katy's bed in the flat that they shared and broke a piece off a bar of chocolate. Her blonde hair showed only the merest hint of strawberry after several washes and was now held in a ponytail with a brightly coloured ribbon covered in cartoon characters. Libby worked on the paediatric ward and instead of uniform they wore practical, colourful tracksuits.

'Hardly.' Katy pulled a face, still hating herself for being so completely tongue-tied when she'd found herself confronted by Jago. 'Lying injured in a hospital bed in a nightie which only has a front to it hardly gives you the confidence to confront your past.'

'Mmm. I see your point.' Libby shook her head. 'I can't believe he's a doctor. I bet none of the female staff get any work done. Is he still fabulous-looking?'

Katy remembered the nurse who'd dropped the chart when he'd walked into the room.

'Spectacular.'

Libby grinned and sucked chocolate from her fingers. 'Oh, boy. What are you going to do?'

Katy lifted a hand and touched the dressing pad on her head. She'd asked herself the same question repeatedly.

'I'm going to start my job and try and ignore the fact that he works there,' she said finally. 'It's a big department and very busy. He's not going to have time to worry about me. It's time I put that episode of my life behind me.'

No more dreams.

'You think you can do that?' Libby chewed slowly, her expression doubtful. 'You were crazy about him, Katy.'

'But he wasn't crazy about me. I was just a conquest. When it came to it, Jago walked away without a backward glance.'

Libby sighed. 'He was a rat, that's true, but, Katy, to be fair to him he never knew about—'

'I don't ever want to talk about that,' Katy interrupted her quickly, and Libby sighed.

'I know, but I think if you told him—'

'It's history.' Katy lifted her chin. 'He left. I'm over it. End of story.'

'Right.' Libby looked at her. 'So you didn't feel a single thing when you looked at him?'

Katy reminded herself of all the reasons she was marrying Freddie.

'No. Not a thing.' She looked at her sister and inhaled deeply. 'I'm not eighteen any more, Lib. Do you really think I'd be mad enough to get involved with him again?'

After all the pain she'd suffered…

'You couldn't help yourself last time,' Libby pointed out gently. 'I saw the way you were with him. He was the one, Katy.'

'I wish you'd stop saying that!' Katy leapt of the bed,

her breathing rapid. 'He wasn't the one. *He wasn't!* I was too young and inexperienced to know what I was doing.'

'Not that young.'

Katy shook her head. 'It can't be love if it's one-sided, and Jago never loved me.'

I don't do commitment, Katy.

'OK, calm down.' Libby looked at her warily and stuck out her hand. 'Have some chocolate. It's good for the nerves.'

Katy sighed. 'I'm beyond chocolate.'

Libby looked unconvinced. 'Nothing is ever beyond the reach of chocolate. Well, if you don't want chocolate, we could go shopping. I saw this gorgeous pair of shoes today.'

Katy gave a wan smile. Libby's two big loves in life were chocolate and shoes. 'If you buy any more shoes we'll need a bigger flat.' She bit her lip. 'I can handle him now, Lib. I'm older and more sensible. I *know* he's wrong for me. I don't want a man like Jago. He's ruthless and macho and totally not my type.'

She remembered the careless way that he'd dismissed the nurse. It seemed that, whatever career he pursued, Jago had to be in control.

'He's Spanish,' Libby reminded her. 'These Mediterranean types are all the same. Unreconstructed when it comes to women.'

'Well, I don't want unreconstructed,' Katy said firmly. 'Not any more. That was just a phase I went through as a teenager. Now I'm older and wiser and I want romantic— like Freddie. Did you see the flowers?'

Libby pulled a face. 'I could hardly miss them. Freddie certainly isn't subtle.'

Katy stiffened defensively. 'He's kind.'

'Right.' Libby looked at her. 'So is the mechanic that services my car, but I'm not marrying him.'

'Just drop it.'

'You know I don't think you should be marrying Freddie, and neither does Alex.' Libby looked her straight in the eye. 'Don't try telling me you're not still affected by Jago, Katy. Look at yourself! You're a nervous wreck. You couldn't resist him before. What makes you think you can do it this time?'

'Because I'm older and wiser and I'm marrying Freddie.'

'Freddie is completely wrong for you.'

Katy gritted her teeth. 'He's very romantic. Something that Jago could never be.'

'But then Jago is one hundred and fifty per cent full-on virile male,' Libby said softly, 'something that Freddie could never be.'

'That's enough!' Katy lifted her hands to her ears but Libby didn't give up.

'You're going to be waking up every morning next to Lord Frederick—that's if he hasn't left early to get to the office before the markets open…'

Katy still had her ears covered. 'I'm not listening.'

'Fine. Don't listen.' Libby sprang off the bed and tossed the chocolate wrapper in the bin. 'But if you think you can work alongside Jago without creating fireworks then you're deluded.'

'I—I can,' Katy stammered. 'He doesn't affect me any more.'

Libby lifted an eyebrow. 'Really?'

'I don't even think about him.'

The heat of his mouth on hers, the erotic sweep of his tongue…

'Right.' Libby looked at her steadily. 'Well, in that case, working with him isn't going to be a problem, is it?'

Two weeks later Katy stood nervously in the A and E department, listening as one of the other consultants showed them round and explained what was expected of them.

A tiny scar hidden in her hairline was the only remaining physical evidence of her accident but emotionally it was a different matter. The shattered pieces of her heart, painstakingly glued back together over the past eleven years, had been torn apart again by just one meeting with Jago.

The air around her felt stuffy and close. *She could hardly breathe.* Just *thinking* about bumping into him made her knees tremble and her palms sweaty.

What had possessed her to think that she could do this?

How would he react when he discovered that she was a doctor and that she was going to be working in his department?

And how was *she* going to react to *him*?

'This is the resuscitation room and it's always kept ready. Basically we divide the department into different areas.' Totally unaware of Katy's inner torment, the consultant smiled at the group of doctors gathered around him. 'For serious injuries we use a team approach in this hospital. It means that different tasks can be performed simultaneously and makes for a more rapid assessment of the patient, and that improves the survival rate.'

Reminding herself that she had a job to do, Katy forced herself to concentrate. It was her first day and at the moment it was quiet, but she'd been warned that there could be an influx of patients at any moment. A group of them had started together and so far everyone seemed friendly enough.

And there was no sign of Jago Rodriguez.

Gradually her knees started to shake a little less and her breathing grew easier.

'How many people make up the trauma team?' A good-looking, fair-haired doctor, who'd introduced himself as Carl Richards, asked the question and the consultant turned to face him.

'We use four doctors, five nurses and a radiographer.

One of the doctors acts as team leader, then there's the airway doctor who does the obvious but also checks the cervical spine and inserts any central or arterial lines that might be needed.'

'And the other two doctors?'

'We call them circulation doctors. They help with the removal of the patients' clothes, put up peripheral lines, insert chest drains—that type of thing. The nurses work in much the same way. The important thing to remember is that there should only be six people touching the patient or it leads to total chaos. The others should keep well back.'

'And most of the senior doctors.' It was Carl again. 'Have they done the ATLS course?'

The consultant nodded. 'The advanced trauma life support course was originated by the American College of Surgeons, but we now run something similar over here in the UK.'

Katy spoke up. 'So will we be part of the trauma team?'

The consultant gave a wry smile. 'You're going to be part of everything. The team leader is always a consultant but you'll certainly be working as circulation doctors, obviously operating within your skill level. If certain procedures are unfamiliar, we expect you to say so. Now, I'm going to show you the most important room of all. The staff common room.'

Half an hour later, Katy pushed her bag into her locker, slammed it shut and made to follow the others out onto the unit. They'd had a cup of coffee and now the work was about to start.

Her first day on A and E.

She was the last person left in the common room and she gave a start as the door crashed open and Jago strode in, formidably male, his strong features strained.

'Tell me this is a joke,' he launched, slamming the door shut behind him and keeping a hand on it so that no one could disturb them. 'I've just seen your name on the rota. *Dr* Katherine Westerling?'

If anything, he was even colder than he'd been when she'd been admitted as a patient and Katy closed her eyes briefly.

Maybe it was her fault. She should have warned him, but when she'd been lying in hospital she hadn't even decided whether she was going to be able to do it.

And now she was having serious doubts.

How could she ever have thought that she could work alongside him without a problem?

Connecting with those volcanic dark eyes, she felt an explosion of awareness erupt inside her body and hated herself for it. It seemed that it didn't matter how indifferent he was to her, she was still a sucker for his type of raw, masculine sexuality.

'It's not a joke.' Katy's breathing was suddenly uneven as she struggled to hide the disturbing effect he had on her. At five feet ten she was used to being at eye level with most men, but she'd always had to look up to Jago. He was six feet three of intimidating, angry male, and being in the same room as him had a seriously detrimental effect on her nerves.

'Why the hell didn't you tell me when you were in here two weeks ago?'

'I—I didn't think it was relevant.'

Because she'd been shell-shocked to see him again.

Because she hadn't made up her mind whether she would be able to take the job, knowing that it would mean working with him.

'Not relevant?' His eyes raked over her in a naked disbelief that would have offended her if she hadn't become used to it over the years. People always looked at her in disbelief because she didn't fit their stereotype of a doctor.

Katy sighed, reading his mind. 'Women become doctors, Jago. Even blondes.'

He frowned sharply. 'I'm not prejudiced against women doctors.'

'So what's wrong?'

'Seeing you in A and E is what's wrong,' he drawled, his penetrating dark gaze locking onto hers. 'You were a model. A woman whose main priority was the state of her nails.'

That wasn't true but she couldn't blame him for thinking that.

At the time she'd been breathlessly aware that Jago had only dated really, *really* beautiful women and she'd been determined to be as beautiful as possible to see off the competition. And that had been time-consuming.

It occurred to her suddenly that she and Jago hadn't ever really talked about anything that mattered. She'd certainly never told him that she'd wanted to be a doctor. In fact, apart from Libby and Alex, no one had known just how badly she'd wanted to be a doctor until the day she'd told her father.

She lifted her chin. 'I gave up modelling when I was eighteen.' *Just after he'd walked out of her life.* 'I—I had a few years off and then I went to medical school.'

He looked at her. 'And did your father approve of that?'

Her heartbeat increased at the memory and her gaze slid away from his. 'No.'

'So you finally stood up to him about something.' He gave a short laugh. 'Good for you. But that still doesn't make you suitable material for an A and E doctor.'

She stiffened, refusing to be intimidated by his disparaging tone. 'I was top of my year, Jago.'

'I never said you weren't bright and I'm sure you'd make an excellent GP,' he said dismissively, his expression hard and uncompromising. 'What was your last job?'

'Paediatrics.'

'Go back there,' he advised silkily. 'Accident and emergency is medicine in the raw. It's a real job. It won't suit you.'

Her heart was thumping so hard she felt dizzy.

'I've done real jobs before.'

'Really?' He lifted an eyebrow, his tone heavy with sarcasm. 'Just how much blood and serious, gut-wrenching trauma have you dealt with in your time, Katy?'

None.

She'd done the required medical and surgical house jobs after she'd qualified, of course, and then she'd done a year of paediatrics before deciding that it wasn't the route she wanted to take in her career.

It had been her consultant on the paediatric ward who'd observed her calm, unflappable nature and suggested that she might like to consider A and E work.

And despite Jago's acid comments, she *knew* she could do it.

'I'll be fine.' She swallowed. If she was honest, she was slightly anxious about how she'd cope with major trauma, but she'd rather stop breathing than admit that to Jago. 'Being a good doctor isn't just about blood and guts. I'm good at communicating with patients and I have good instincts when it comes to judging clinical situations.'

His eyes raked over her from head to foot, taking in every inch of her appearance. 'And do you really think that scraping back that blonde hair, wearing glasses that you don't need and dressing like my grandmother is going to make you seem tougher?'

Katy touched the glasses self-consciously. Having long blonde hair and being considered exceptionally pretty had turned out to be a distinct disadvantage, so over the years she'd adopted a disguise. She'd discovered that if she dressed discreetly then people paid more attention to what she was saying. But not Jago, of course. He saw through the disguise right to her soul. He'd always been razor sharp.

She decided to be honest. 'I wear the glasses because they make people take me more seriously.'

His laugh was unsympathetic. 'And I bet you need all the help you can get, *querida*.'

She bristled at his tone and lifted her chin with an icy dignity that she'd learned from her mother.

'I'm a good doctor, Jago.' She'd had to prove it on umpteen occasions in the past so it was nothing new. 'I'll be fine.'

'Too right you'll be fine.' His voice was lethally soft and contained more than a hint of menace. 'You'll be fine because I'm going to be breathing down your neck every minute of the day. Everything you do, Katy, every patient you see, I'm going to be there, next to you, watching. I do not need another lightweight doctor in this department. If someone is sick on those designer shoes of yours, you're going to have to carry on to the end of the shift. You're going to have to prove yourself to me. And you don't have to be as good as everyone else, you have to be twice as good. Or you're out.'

Her heart was thumping double time.

'I'm not lightweight. You're making judgements about me—'

'Based on experience.' He moved towards her. 'I know you, Katy. I know how you think. You hate confrontation. There's no way you'll cope with A and E. I guarantee that after one week you'll wish you were back in paediatrics.'

She licked her lips, her whole body pulsating in response to his looming proximity.

'That won't happen and you're totally wrong about me.'

'Yes?' His black eyes were as hard as flint. 'When I knew you, you didn't even have the courage to stand up to your own father. You were terrified that he might find out you were seeing me.'

She tried to back away but there was nowhere to go. The cold metal of the lockers pressed through the thin fabric of her blouse.

It was true that at eighteen she'd been terrified of her father. And as it had turned out, her fear had been fully justified.

But Jago didn't know that, of course. He'd vanished into the sunset before any of it could get ugly, ignorant of the devastation he'd left behind him.

He'd never known what her father was like.

Very few people did.

'Your father was a tough man—probably still is—but he's a walk in the park compared to some of the patients we see in this department on a Saturday night.'

A walk in the park?

Remembering just what had transpired after Jago had left, Katy was shocked into speechlessness.

He stepped closer. 'You don't like disagreements or controversy and you hate all forms of violence. We do violence quite well in A and E, you know.' His tone was smooth. 'Saturday afternoons after football and rugby, nights after the pubs close. What are you going to do when the department is full of drunks? What are you going to do when someone turns round and hits you?'

He was trying to scare her off but it wasn't going to work.

The only thing that frightened her about working in A and E was being close to *him*.

Especially the way he was acting at the moment.

Like a madman.

As if he wasn't the man who'd taken her virginity and then walked away without a backward glance.

She cast him a confused look. 'Why are you being like this?'

His gaze was hard and unsympathetic. 'Because this is a horrifically busy department and frankly I don't have time to nursemaid someone who's main concern in life is whether she needs to file her nails.'

He made her sound frivolous and shallow, but maybe she'd seemed that way to him when he'd known her at eighteen. One thing was sure, if they were ever going to be able to work together effectively, they had to get the past out of the way.

'You don't know me any more.' She kept her tone conciliatory, the way she did when her father was in one of his scary moods. 'It's been eleven years since you last saw me. Maybe we should talk about what happened, Jago.'

Maybe he could explain why he'd walked away.

Jago's eyes were cold and his broad shoulders were rigid with tension. 'The past is history. There's nothing that I want to talk about and if you're trying to convince me that you've changed, you're wasting your breath. You're forgetting that I met the man you're engaged to.' He gave a short laugh. 'That in itself was enough to prove to me that you haven't changed one little bit.'

Maybe *he* had changed, she reflected. Despite his Spanish ancestry, Jago had always been so emotionally controlled that in the past she'd longed to do something which would shake him out of his almost permanent state of indifference. Yet she sensed that at this moment he was hanging onto control by little more than a thread. For the first time she was seeing a hint of that volatility that was supposed to characterise Mediterranean men.

But what she didn't understand was *why*. Something had obviously really challenged his legendary cool and she had absolutely no idea what. And his lack of remorse about the way he'd treated her still puzzled her. He seemed so *hard*.

She forced her mind back to the subject. 'You don't know anything about Freddie.'

'I know he's the man your father's chosen for you.' That burning dark gaze locked on hers with all the lethal accuracy of a deadly weapon. As he stepped even closer to her his voice dropped to a low purr, like a tiger soothing its prey before the kill. 'Does he make you hot inside, Katy? Does he make you so desperate that he has you panting and ripping at his clothes?'

Powerful images exploded in her head and her face burned with shock and embarrassment at his explicit words.

'Have you finished?' Determined not to betray just how uncomfortable she felt, she looked him straight in the eye. It was a mistake.

She tumbled into the fathomless depths of his dark eyes and felt her knees tremble.

He leaned forward. 'That man has no idea how to unlock the real Katy.'

'And I suppose you think you do!'

'Of course.' The lazy arrogance in his voice was the final straw and she lifted a hand and slapped him so hard that the palm of her hand stung.

'*Dios mio.*' His head jerked backwards and he looked at her with raw incredulity, disbelief pulsating in the depths of his eyes.

Stunned by her own behaviour, Katy opened her mouth to apologise and then closed it again. There was no way she was apologising to him!

'Eleven years is a long time, Jago, and you don't know anything about who I am any more.' Her small hands clenched by her sides and she forced herself to breathe normally. 'I'm more than capable of working in this department and I'm going to marry Freddie.'

They stood, eyes trapped by an invisible force, until the

door opened and a male voice said, 'I've found our strag-gler. She's still in the common room.'

The consultant walked in and gave Jago a nod before turning to Katy. Fortunately he didn't seem to notice the reddened streak on Jago's cheekbone.

'If you've finished in here, I'll take you out and see which member of staff you're allocated to. We find that the new casualty officers settle in quickly if they work closely with another member of staff. I'll just check who that is.'

'You needn't bother.' Jago's voice was soft and his eyes were still fixed on Katy's pale face. 'Dr Westerling will be working with me.'

His colleague looked startled. 'Oh, right—well, you've obviously already met Jago Rodriguez, one of our other consultants. In that case, I'll leave you in his capable hands. I'm sure you're keen to get started.'

Jago's mouth curled into a smile. 'I'm sure Dr Westerling can't wait.'

There was a sardonic gleam in his sexy dark eyes that brought a flush to her pale cheeks and a sick feeling to the pit of her stomach.

Working with Jago wasn't just going to be difficult.

It was going to be a nightmare.

Twenty-four hours later Katy was wondering why she'd ever thought she'd be able to cope with A and E.

She'd seen a never-ending stream of patients, most of them angry at having been kept waiting for hours.

'Can't we see patients any faster?' she asked Charlotte, the sister who had looked after her when she'd been brought in after her car accident. 'I'm fed up with being verbally abused by everyone I see.'

'Welcome to A and E.' Charlotte handed her a set of X-rays to check. 'We make a dent and then an emergency comes in and takes priority. That's the way it works. That's why we have triage. Non-emergency cases go to the bottom of the pile and they stay there until someone has time to see them.' She smiled sympathetically at Katy's drawn expression. 'Don't worry, you get used to people yelling at you after a while.'

'I don't mind people yelling,' Katy lied quickly, not wanting to risk Charlotte telling Jago that she couldn't cope. 'I just wish we didn't have to keep people waiting.'

'At least you're working with Jago. He can be a pretty hard taskmaster, I know, but he's a brilliant doctor. You're lucky.'

Katy kept her mouth clamped shut. Lucky? She certainly didn't feel lucky to be working with Jago. She felt as though she must have done something seriously wrong in a previous life to have deserved such punishment.

Realising that Charlotte was looking at her oddly, she managed a smile.

'I'm sure you're right,' she replied smoothly. 'I'm looking forward to learning from him.'

'As a doctor he's staggeringly gifted,' Charlotte went on. 'He has this uncanny ability to spot things that other people miss, but sometimes he forgets that the rest of us are human. Don't let him get to you.'

He *was* getting to her.

He made it perfectly obvious that he didn't think she had what it took to work in A and E and he was watching her every move, waiting for her to make a mistake.

Why did he hate her so much?

All she'd ever done had been to fall in love with him, and surely that was her problem, not his.

They hadn't really talked about what had happened in the past. Maybe she should bring it up. Clear the air.

Feeling totally miserable, Katy sighed and reached for the X-rays but at that moment Annie, one of the staff nurses, rushed up.

'Ambulance Control just rang. They're bringing in a forty-year-old man who's had an accident in a warehouse. He got caught by a forklift truck. Apparently he's in a bad way. Very weak pulse and virtually no blood pressure. They should be here in less than five minutes.'

'Find Jago,' Charlotte said immediately, but his voice came from behind them.

'I heard. Annie, get the trauma team together in Resus and make sure we have a radiographer. I don't want to be hanging around for X-rays.' His gaze flickered to Katy. 'You can join us in Resus and act as one of the circulation doctors. You saw us in action yesterday—do you think you can cope?'

Katy's stomach lurched and her pulse rate quickened, but she met his gaze without flinching.

'Of course.'

She'd cope or die in the attempt.

'Good.' His dark eyes locked on hers moodily and then he strode off towards Resus, leaving her to follow.

Charlotte alerted the nursing team and one of them was given the task of informing people in the waiting room that the waiting time was likely to be increased because a major injury was coming in.

'There'll be a riot,' Annie predicted gloomily, and Harry, one of the other consultants, nodded.

'Very probably, but there isn't much we can do about it except mop up the blood afterwards.'

Jago was prowling around Resus, checking that the right equipment was ready and everything was where he wanted it.

Moments later the doors crashed open and the paramedics hurried in with the stretcher.

'This is Dan Walker. He's a warehouse supervisor. He was caught under the ribs by a forklift truck. No obvious injury but he's shocked and his pulse is thready. We've given him high-flow oxygen and we managed to get a line in at the scene…'

The paramedic outlined the care they'd given and Jago moved to the head of the trolley.

'OK, let's move him across, on my count—one two three.'

They lifted the man carefully and he groaned slightly, his skin pale and clammy.

Katy's blood was pounding in her veins. This was her first real trauma case. What if she did something wrong?

But it soon became clear to her that she couldn't possibly do anything wrong because Jago was directing the entire operation with an air of cool command which left no doubt in anyone's mind who was in charge.

Having secured the man's airway and satisfied himself that there was no damage to the cervical spine, he turned his attention to the work of the rest of the team.

'Get another line in. I want vital signs recorded every five minutes and get his clothes off fast—I want every inch of him examined.'

Using sharp scissors, they cut off his clothes and Katy reached for the man's wrist to insert another line. One of the nurses handed her a swab and venflon and she searched frantically for a vein.

'Everything's shutting down,' she murmured, her fingers slipping on the man's skin as she nervously tried to find a vein.

'Let Harry try,' Jago said sharply, and she gritted her teeth and felt around again for a vein.

'Give me one more go—I think I felt something then.'

Please—*please*…

Something moved under her fingers. Was that it?

She slid the needle through the skin and breathed a sigh of relief as blood came back into the venflon.

'I've done it. I'm in.'

'Well done.' Harry gave her an encouraging smile but Jago merely barked out more instructions.

'Take blood for group and cross-match, full blood count, urea and electrolytes, and get a catheter in so that we can assess his fluid output. What's his blood pressure doing?'

'It's falling.' Annie checked the reading and recorded it on the chart.

'Remember that there is a consistent fall in the systolic blood pressure only after 30 per cent of blood volume is lost,' Jago said, his tone cool. 'Get him attached to an ECG monitor and let's give him a bolus of fluid. Start with a litre of warm colloid and then we'll reassess.'

There were so many questions that Katy wanted to ask but she knew they were going to have to wait until the patient was stable.

She watched while Jago examined the patient's abdomen, his hands moving skilfully as he looked for signs of tenderness.

'There's bruising and tenderness under the ribs,' he murmured, and then glanced at Annie. 'Phone down and see if they've confirmed the blood group yet. It's been ten minutes so they should have. Once they have, get some blood up here,' he ordered sharply, and Annie hurried to the phone just as another nurse popped her head round the door.

'His wife is in the relatives' room. Is there someone who can see her?'

Jago glanced at Charlotte. 'Can one of your team go to her until we've stabilised him? Tell her we'll be with her as soon as we have some news.'

Charlotte moved towards the door. 'And if she wants to come and see him?'

Jago didn't hesitate. 'Then let her.'

Katy frowned and Jago raised an eyebrow in her direction.

'Something wrong, Katy?'

At least he was calling her by her first name now, instead of referring to her as 'Dr Westerling'. 'I just thought it might be distressing for her to see him like this.'

'It is distressing…' Jago glanced across to check the ECG and the blood-pressure reading '…but studies have shown that on balance it's probably better for the relatives to see the patient in Resus than not to see them.'

Annie looked up. 'His blood pressure is falling, Jago.'

'He needs blood and we need to call the surgeons and warn them that he's likely to need a laparotomy.'

Jago looked impatiently towards the door and at that moment one of the nurses came hurrying in, carrying the blood bags.

'At last.' Jago reached out a hand and took one of the blood bags, attaching it quickly to the giving set. 'Open the tap and let's see if that helps.'

They worked to stabilise the man but the blood transfusion seemed to have no effect.

'Still no improvement. OK, that tells us one of two things.' Jago's expression was grim. 'Either the shock isn't caused by bleeding, or he's bleeding faster than we can infuse the blood—my money's on the latter. He needs urgent surgical intervention. Has someone bleeped the surgeons?'

Charlotte nodded. 'Mr Hart is on his way.'

'Well, he'd better be quick.' Jago turned his attention back to the patient, who was deteriorating by the minute.

'His blood pressure is still falling.' Annie looked at Jago expectantly and his mouth tightened.

'Push that blood through faster.'

At that moment the door swung open and a tall, blond man strode into the room. 'Jago?'

Jago gave a succinct report on the man's condition and the surgeon examined him briefly.

'You're right. He's bleeding. Let's take him straight to Theatre.'

There was a flurry of activity and the man was transferred to the operating theatre for a laparotomy which would allow the surgeons to assess any internal damage.

Katy found herself alone in Resus with Charlotte. 'Phew, what a mess!' She glanced around the room, taking in the discarded blood bags, needles and other equipment.

'What happens now?'

'We clear it up ready for the next patient,' Charlotte said immediately, thrusting needles into the sharps bin and scooping up soiled dressings. 'Jago's gone to talk to the relatives with Annie. Can I ask you something?'

'Of course.' Katy checked the intubation tray and ran another bag of saline through a giving set.

'How do you two know each other?'

Katy's eyes flew to hers and she thought about denying their past acquaintance, but Charlotte's next words made her realise the futility of that approach.

'When you were brought in here two weeks ago, he was the one who identified you.'

'Oh.' Katy concentrated on the equipment she was checking, wondering what Jago had felt when he'd seen her lying on the ambulance stretcher. Had he felt any guilt at all? 'We knew each other years ago. He used to work for my father.'

'In the bank?' Charlotte's eyes widened. 'He's filthy rich and we've all been dying to know how he made his money. I suppose that answers the question.'

'I suppose so.'

Katy moved away, hoping that was the end of it. She hated gossiping about people.

Charlotte was still looking at her in fascination. 'Did you know him well?'

Katy shook her head and avoided eye contact. 'Not that well.'

She'd thought that there had been gentleness under the strength but she'd been wrong.

Charlotte gave a wistful sigh. 'He's the hospital heart-throb.'

Katy kept her eyes fixed on the intubation tray. Of course he was. Jago Rodriguez was seriously rich, stunningly good-looking and single. A prime target for every woman on the planet.

Except her.

She'd learned her lesson the hard way eleven years ago and she wasn't that innocent, naïve girl anymore.

Charlotte sighed. 'Every available woman in the hospital dreams of being the one to tame him and marry him.'

Katy looked up at that, unable to hide her incredulous expression. 'Marry him?' Well that showed how well they knew Jago. *I don't do commitment, Katy.* 'If you know him then you'll know he isn't the marrying kind.'

Charlotte shrugged. 'Everyone's the marrying kind if they meet the right person.'

'I don't think so.' Katy's voice was soft and thoughtful. 'I think some people just can't allow themselves to be that vulnerable.'

And Jago didn't have a vulnerable part to his make-up.

At one point she'd thought he had. He'd fooled her with a display of gentleness that had turned her insides to jelly but she knew now that that was just part of his superior bedroom technique.

'You've obviously thought about it a lot.' Charlotte hung the giving set over the stand and looked at her quizzically. 'But you're getting married so you must believe in love and commitment.'

Did she?

Katy turned her attention back to the intubation tray, not wanting to shatter Charlotte's romantic illusions.

She certainly wasn't in love with Freddie.

And she didn't feel guilty about it because she knew that Freddie wasn't in love with her either. He was marrying her because she was the right sort of girl with the right sort of connections and that suited her fine. She didn't want love.

Her one experience of love had been a shattering, all-consuming experience that had threatened her very existence.

I don't do commitment, Katy.

'Not that we hospital staff really get a look in,' Charlotte said gloomily, tearing off her plastic apron and lobbing it in the bin. 'He's dating a stunning Brazilian model at the moment. The real woman type. Legs up to her armpits and boobs to make a man drool. She's a very lucky woman.'

Katy clenched her fists and told herself firmly that she didn't care who Jago was dating. It was none of her business.

And she wanted to end the conversation.

'I'd better get back to the main area and see some more patients,' she said quickly, anxious to get away from Charlotte. She was nice but she didn't need to talk about Jago. Working with him and seeing him every day was bad enough without talking about him as well.

CHAPTER FOUR

KATY'S first week passed quickly and every time she looked up Jago seemed to be there, challenging her, asking questions, his handsome face inscrutable.

Determined not to make a mistake, she examined every patient meticulously, made sure that her questions were detailed, never took anything at face value. And in her opinion she'd performed well. But Jago hadn't uttered a single word of praise and she was starting to feel the strain.

Was he going to keep this up indefinitely?

Did he really think that she wasn't up to the pressures of A and E or did he have another reason for not wanting her in his department.

A more personal reason perhaps?

On her first Saturday night working on A and E a fight broke out in the street behind the hospital. They heard the sound of police sirens and a few minutes later a group of drunks staggered through the door that led to the ambulance bay, half-supporting a man who seemed barely conscious.

'Hey, you!' One of the drunks waved a hand at Charlotte who frowned with distaste.

'You can't come in through that entrance,' she said tightly. 'It's reserved for emergency vehicles. You need to—'

'Don't tell me what I can and can't do,' the man slurred, his eyes flashing angrily at Charlotte as he struggled to remain upright and focus. 'Get me a bloody doctor. *Now!*'

Charlotte stiffened and turned to Jago expectantly.

'This is one for Katy,' he delivered softly, his dark eyes connecting with Katy's in unmistakable challenge.

There was no missing the message in his gaze. This was

one of the situations he was convinced she'd never be able to deal with, and he was testing her.

She almost laughed. She'd probably had more experience with drunk, violent men than he had.

Ignoring Charlotte's shocked murmur of protest, Katy stepped forward, her manner calm and professional.

'That looks like a nasty cut.'

She addressed her remarks directly to the injured man, who barely acknowledged her presence.

His head rolled onto his chest and his expression was glazed.

Was he drunk or was he suffering the consequences of a head injury?

She'd read enough to be aware of the potential pitfalls of dismissing someone as drunk. There were plenty of horror stories about people who'd been discharged from Casualty only to die the next day as a result of a head injury that no one had taken seriously. Drink could mask a number of symptoms and she had no intention of missing anything.

She turned to his friend, who was clearly having trouble staying upright. 'What's his name?'

'James.'

'And what happened?'

The man swayed slightly. 'He fell over and banged his head.'

He was slurring his words so badly that it was difficult to understand him, but Katy knew how important it was to obtain some sort of history. 'And did he knock himself out?'

The man shrugged, his eyes glazed. 'Dunno.'

Great. Some history.

'All right.' Katy's tone was brisk. 'Well, I need to take a look at his head. Why don't you sit him over there and then go and give his details to Reception?'

The man didn't answer, his body swaying as he watched her. 'I asked for a doctor. You're never a doctor.'

Katy gave a calm smile. The same smile she'd used on her father time and time again.

Don't antagonise him, Katy.

'I'm a doctor.' She spoke quietly, knowing better than to joke or argue with him or enter into any conversation that wasn't necessary. She could see that the man was very drunk and suspected that he was only too keen to pick a fight. 'Now, if you'll just sit him over here, I can take a look at his head.'

Without giving the man time to argue, she took charge and helped the injured man onto the couch in the first cubicle, half-drawing the curtain around him.

She looked at Charlotte. 'Would you mind showing his friend the way to Reception so that he can give some details, please?'

Charlotte nodded, her eyes wide with admiration. 'Of course.'

Jago said nothing. He just leaned broad shoulders against the wall, his eyes narrowed as he watched Katy.

Trying to hide how much his presence affected her, Katy reached for an ophthalmoscope to examine the patient's eyes, but as she put a hand on the man's head, he gave a groan and lurched towards her. She sidestepped neatly and he vomited over the floor.

Katy reached for a bowl and held it for the man while he retched and mumbled incoherently.

Charlotte, back from Reception, rolled her eyes in disgust. 'It's on your shoes,' she muttered, and Katy shook her head dismissively.

'I'll sort that out later.' She didn't care about her shoes but she was seriously worried about her patient. Were the symptoms he was displaying the result of alcohol or the bang on the head he'd received? It was such a difficult decision.

If she admitted a patient who was perfectly healthy, she'd be wasting precious hospital resources. On the other hand, if she discharged him and his symptoms were the result of a serious head injury, she would have failed in her duty as a doctor.

Medicine had never seemed so complicated.

She knew that she could ask Jago for advice but she didn't want to. He might take it as a sign of weakness on her part and she was determined to prove to him that she was more than capable of doing the job without constant supervision.

'Can you hear me? Can you tell me your name?'

She spoke clearly and the man groaned and mumbled something unintelligible.

'Do you know what day it is?'

She continued to question the man but was far from satisfied by the results.

Jago stepped closer to her. 'He could just be very drunk,' he said coolly, and she knew he was testing her again.

'Or his symptoms could be the result of his head injury.' She tried to ignore the explosion of heat that consumed her body as he moved closer still. Breathing in his warm, familiar, male scent, she felt her head swim.

'So which is it, Dr Westerling?'

She made the mistake of looking at him and his eyes locked onto hers with the power and force of a missile attack.

The mood was suddenly electric and Katy found herself mesmerised by the look of raw, sexual intimacy in his eyes.

Suddenly her breathing was suspended and she struggled to find her voice.

'I—I need to finish my examination before I can answer that question.'

He dealt her a slanting smile. The same smile that she'd found totally irresistible at the age of eighteen. 'Then finish it, Doctor.'

Cursing her own weakness and the effect he had on her, Katy turned her attention back to the patient.

She asked more questions, checked the patient's reflexes and only after completing an exhaustive examination did she make her decision.

'I'm sending him for a CT scan and then I'm admitting him,' she said firmly, and Jago lifted an eyebrow.

'And why is that?'

'He's showing symptoms of a serious head injury. Headache, vomiting, disorientation. I'm not prepared to discharge him.'

Confident in her decision, Katy looked straight at him, her heart lifting as she saw the glimmer of respect in his dark eyes.

Finally.

After a week of concentrated hard work.

'Good decision,' he said smoothly. 'Make the arrangements and then come to my office and we can talk about it further.'

Light-headed with relief that she'd done the right thing, Katy suddenly wanted to smile. *He'd praised her.* He thought she'd done a good job.

But there was no way she was going to his office.

The effect he had on her was just too powerful and if she couldn't control her reactions she needed to avoid him.

She lifted her chin, her confidence increasing by the moment. *She'd done a good job.* 'Can we talk about it tomorrow, please? I was supposed to be off duty an hour ago and I'm going out so I need to go and clean the vomit off my shoes and—' her eyes challenged his and a small smile touched her mouth '—file my nails.'

And remind herself that dreaming of Jago was a fast route to a miserable life.

Jago looked taken aback. Then to her surprise he threw back his dark head and laughed. 'Tomorrow will be fine.' He turned to Charlotte, who was gaping at the scene being played out before her. 'I'm out of here. If you need me, call my mobile.'

Charlotte watched him stride away and looked at her with awe. 'Would someone mind telling me what's going on here? You answered him back and he just laughed,' she muttered, reaching for the notes so that she could make the arrangements for the CT scan. 'And I can't believe he let you deal with those drunks. I've never known him to act like that before. Normally he's very protective of the female staff, to the point of chauvinism. I mean, we all ought to deal with the same patients but the truth is when you're built like Jago you stand more chance with a violent drunk than someone who is built like you. I don't know what he was playing at.'

Katy gave a weak smile. She knew exactly what he'd been playing at. He'd been waiting for her to fail.

He'd wanted her to fail since the day she'd started.

What she didn't understand was why.

A pleasant warmth spread through her veins. His reasons didn't really matter. *She hadn't failed.* She'd managed fine, she knew she had. She'd made all the right clinical decisions and she hadn't needed his help.

She straightened her slim shoulders and gave a small smile, suddenly feeling more confident.

He'd tested her and she'd passed with flying colours.

So now what would happen?

Jago closed the door of his office and ran long fingers through his cropped hair.

What the hell was the matter with him?

He'd sent a woman to deal with a bunch of drunks.

And not just any woman, he'd sent Katy. Katy, who was about as robust as a spring flower.

What had he been thinking of?

But he knew the answer to that, of course.

He'd been trying to prove that she couldn't cope with the rigours of practising medicine in the A and E department. He'd been trying to scare her away.

Because he didn't want her here, on his territory, looking at him with those wide violet-blue eyes.

Just thinking of her exceptionally beautiful, heart-shaped face made him harden in an instinctive and powerful male reaction, and he gave an exclamation of disgust.

Hadn't he learned anything? Was he really that basic that he could forget everything just to satisfy the most primitive of male urges?

What was it about Katy Westerling? True, she was astonishingly beautiful but he met beautiful women all the time and they didn't make him abandon his usual caution towards members of the opposite sex.

He had to keep reminding himself that she wasn't what she seemed.

That the innocent aura that aroused a man's most fiercely protective instincts was actually just an act.

His hands tightened into fists and his hard jaw clenched as he remembered the photographs her father had shown him.

She might have been a virgin when he'd first slept with her, but less than four weeks later she'd slept with another man.

I love you, Jago.

Remembering the incredibly intimate pictures he'd seen, he growled low in his throat and strolled across to the window of his office which looked out on the ambulance bay.

It was eleven years ago, he reminded himself. And eleven years was a long time. Enough to change a person, and Katy had obviously changed.

The old Katy had been deliciously shy and tongue-tied but the Katy he'd seen in action today was very different from the girl he'd made love to so long ago. Far from buckling under the challenge he'd set her, she'd coped well.

In fact, she'd handled those drunks with an admirable level of skill and tact. There had been every sign that they could have become violent at any minute but she'd reacted with textbook efficiency and had successfully defused any suggestion of aggression on the part of the patient and his friends.

She'd behaved as though she'd been operating totally within her comfort zone, which didn't make a scrap of sense. When would Katy Westerling, with her over-privileged, protected upbringing, ever have been exposed to drunk, violent men?

His dark brows locked in a frown as he puzzled over her complete lack of concern. She hadn't even seemed to notice the danger. But some deep-seated instinct told him that she had been all too aware and had known exactly how to cope with it. She'd stood up to them and she'd stood up to him.

He allowed himself a brief smile of admiration as he remembered her gutsy response to his command that she meet him in his office.

She'd remembered his caustic remark about her filing her nails and she'd thrown it back at him.

No, Katy had definitely changed. She'd dropped the in-nocent act—and they both knew that it had been nothing more than an act—and she was showing a level of courage that frankly surprised him. There were still hints of the feminine fragility that she'd shown at eighteen, but he sensed a strength and determination that hadn't been there before.

Suddenly he was intrigued.

And he was also impressed. He'd seen numerous col-leagues make the mistake of dismissing a patient who was drunk. She hadn't made that mistake. Even when the patient had vomited on what he assumed to be a frighteningly ex-pensive pair of shoes, she hadn't allowed it to cloud her decision-making.

She was a good doctor.

And he had to face the fact that the reason he was being so hard on her had absolutely nothing to do with her clinical abilities and everything to do with his own emotions.

* * *

Katy was nearly at the end of her shift the following day when a call came through requesting a medical team to attend an accident.

'They've got a man trapped in a car and they're worried about his leg. I'm the duty consultant so it's mine,' Jago said immediately, reaching for high-visibility jackets and the equipment they'd need at the roadside. 'I'll take Charlotte and Katy.'

Katy felt the adrenaline rush through her veins.

She knew that immediate care—tending to the patient at the scene of the accident—was very different from looking after someone in the A and E department where they were surrounded by equipment.

Was he expecting her to take the lead as he had with the drunken head-injury patient the previous day?

'I'm taking you as an observer,' he said smoothly, evidently reading her mind, 'and an extra pair of hands if we need one. I'll be right by your side all the time.'

And she was supposed to find that reassuring?

But Katy didn't have time to reflect on Jago's reasons for taking her because they were soon in the car, travelling at high speed towards the scene of the accident.

The roads were slick with rain and Jago drove fast but carefully, the powerful headlights cutting through the darkness.

They arrived to find the fire crew cutting one of the occupants of the car out of the vehicle.

Jago retrieved several rucksacks from the car and checked that she was wearing the correct protective clothing.

The darkness and the foul weather were clearly hampering the rescue efforts.

Responding to a shout from one of the paramedics, Katy hurried across to one of the stretchers.

'We've got him on a spinal board and he's conscious but

his leg's a mess. It needs attention before we transfer him.'
The paramedics addressed her directly and Katy looked
frantically around for Jago but he was speaking to a member of the fire crew.

Which meant it was up to her.

A blanket was covering the injured man and Katy lifted
it gently, feeling the colour drain out of her face as she saw
the extent of the man's injuries. The leg was severely de-
formed and she felt a cold rush of panic in her chest. *Where
should she start?* She could see that there was an open
fracture, with part of the bone exposed to the air, as well
as a severe laceration. She knew that it was important to
cover it to try and prevent infection but the leg was so badly
damaged that she was afraid of making the damage worse.

Aware that she was well outside her own realms of experience, she looked over her shoulder for Jago and to her
relief he was there, his powerful presence reassuring in the
chaos of the accident.

'What have we got?'

Unlike her, his expression didn't flicker as he saw the
state of the man's leg. He merely pulled on a pair of sterile
gloves, and turned to the nearest paramedic and quietly
listed the equipment he needed.

Katy took a deep breath to steady her stomach and those
sharp dark eyes settled on her face.

'Are you OK?' He frowned sharply as he scanned her
pale face. 'You can wait in the car if you like.'

And give him more ammunition for accusing her of not
being able to cope? No way!

'I'm fine,' Katy replied sickly, hoping that he couldn't
see just how much she was shaking.

'As long as you're sure.' His voice was surprisingly gentle. 'If you change your mind, let me know.'

The rain had plastered his jet-black hair to his face and
trickled off the dark stubble on his hard jaw.

He was breathtakingly handsome and very much in control of the situation.

Which was a relief because she felt completely and totally out of her depth.

He kept his voice low, explaining what he was doing as he worked. And he worked quickly.

'Normally we wouldn't handle the injured part without splinting,' he told her after they'd given the man drugs to control the pain, 'but in this case there's severe deformity and the blood supply is compromised.'

'So that could damage the soft tissues?'

'Exactly. A good blood supply is vital to limb survival. So in this case I'm going to apply gentle traction to restore the alignment of the bones. Then we'll splint.'

Katy blinked in surprise as one of the paramedics took a Polaroid photograph of the wound before covering it with a sterile dressing.

'Why did he do that?' She spoke in a low voice even though the patient was drifting in and out of consciousness, barely aware of what was happening.

'Because exposing the wound again in the A and E department will increase the risk of infection, so if we can we take a photo at the roadside before we cover it,' Jago explained. 'No one will disturb the dressing now until this chap reaches Theatre.'

Katy watched while he reduced the fracture and then checked the pulses in the limb.

'OK.' He glanced up at the paramedics and ran a hand over his face to clear his vision, his thick, dark lashes clumped together in the rain. 'I need a long leg splint.'

They produced one immediately and Jago immobilised the leg with help from Katy and one of the paramedics.

'Splinting the leg will help control the pain but we need to get him to hospital fast. Blood loss from limb wounds and internal bleeding from fractures contribute to shock so we need to resuscitate him carefully.' His eyes flickered to

Katy. 'Don't forget that blood loss from open fractures can be two or three times greater than that from closed fractures.'

Katy listened, taking in everything he was saying, totally in awe of his amazing calm and the amount of knowledge he displayed.

He seemed totally indifferent to the rain and darkness, acting with the same degree of supreme self-confidence that he displayed in the well-equipped A and E department.

He was talking again. 'One of the advantages of attending the scene of the accident is that you get a real picture of what happened and that helps you assess the possible injuries.'

She was eager to learn from him and for a brief moment their past history was forgotten, the tension between them easing as they concentrated on the patient. 'And that's why you always question the paramedics about whether the patient was a passenger or the driver?'

Jago nodded, his attention fixed on the patient. 'It's important to know whether they were in the vehicle or a pedestrian. Whether they were restrained by a seat belt. The direction of impact and the degree of damage to the car.'

'So if you know that someone was thrown from a vehicle—'

'Then you know that you're dealing with potentially fatal injuries,' he slotted in, nodding to the paramedics to indicate that they could load the patient into the ambulance. 'It's one of the reasons we always make you undress trauma patients in the A and E department. You never know what injuries may be hiding and clinical signs may be subtle, particularly in the unconscious patient.'

He directed operations as the patient was carefully lifted into the ambulance and then sprang into the vehicle, his movements swift and athletic.

'You and Charlotte bring the car. I'll see you back in A and E.'

She turned back to the car feeling a huge range of emotions. On the one hand she felt that she'd learned a lot but on the other she felt helpless and cross with herself, knowing that she hadn't dealt with the situation well.

The truth was, she'd been horrified by the extent of the injuries she'd seen and too panicked to know where to begin.

Was that normal?

Had other doctors found themselves in the same situation?

Charlotte walked up to her, carrying some equipment. 'Slick, isn't he?'

Katy helped her lift it into the boot of the car. 'He's very confident.'

'Well, that's because he knows what he's doing.' Charlotte slammed the boot shut. 'He's ferociously intelligent and he never loses his cool.'

Except with her.

Katy walked round the car and slid into the passenger seat, relieved to get out of the rain.

What would happen now? He'd been waiting for signs that she couldn't cope with trauma work and unfortunately she'd now given him all the ammunition he needed. The way he'd looked at her had left her in absolutely no doubt that he'd noticed her horrified reaction. Hardly an impressive response for a doctor who was beginning a career in accident and emergency medicine, she thought, frustrated beyond belief by what she perceived as her own weakness.

Her first experience of on-scene trauma and she'd panicked and behaved like a frightened rabbit.

He had every right to be impatient with her.

As she and Charlotte drove back towards the hospital, she pondered on the outcome of the inevitable encounter. He'd said that if she couldn't prove herself then she'd be out.

So what would happen now?

CHAPTER FIVE

JAGO heard the tap on the door of his office and looked up from his computer with a frown.

He'd had a long and trying day and technically he was now off duty so he hadn't been expecting visitors.

Katy stood in the doorway, her blue eyes wary as she watched him from the doorway.

She looked tired and incredibly nervous.

He sat back in his chair, his eyes suddenly watchful, his senses on full alert. Why was she nervous? She was looking at him the way a baby impala looked at a hungry lion at lunchtime.

She closed the door behind her and cleared her throat. 'I didn't mean to disturb you.' Faint streaks of colour touched her cheekbones and for a disturbing moment he had an all too clear recollection of the way she'd looked after he'd finally made love to her the first time.

Flushed, round-eyed, softly feminine and in awe of him—much the way she was looking right now.

He felt his body harden in response and he felt a rush of anger at his own inability to control his reactions around her.

'I'm in the middle of something so I'd appreciate it if you could make it quick.'

He saw her flinch but steeled himself against feeling sympathy, reminding himself that she wasn't as gentle and innocent as she seemed.

As he'd discovered to his cost.

'I just wanted to apologise for earlier,' she said quietly, her fingers digging into her palms. 'I was useless out there. I don't know what happened. I'm sorry…'

He was so utterly captivated by her soft mouth that it took him a moment to understand what she was talking about.

The accident. He shook himself slightly. She was talking about the accident.

'You weren't useless.' He resolutely pushed away memories of all that stunning blonde hair spread over the soft grass as he'd rolled her underneath him on a baking summer's day eleven years earlier.

'I wasn't prepared for the injury to be so severe,' she confessed shakily. 'I—I've never attended the scene of an accident before. I didn't know what to do, and I'm sorry.'

He sat back in his chair, suddenly understanding why she was so nervous. Hadn't he warned her on her first day that if she didn't perform she'd be out? She was afraid that her shocked reaction to her first exposure to major trauma at the roadside would count against her.

She was afraid that he was going to get rid of her.

And that had certainly been his intention when he'd first realised that she was going to be working in his department.

He hadn't thought she'd last five minutes.

He hadn't *wanted* her to last five minutes.

And he'd been incredibly hard on her. Harder on her than any other doctor in his team.

And she'd surprised him. So far she'd proved herself to be thorough and competent, and he'd observed on several occasions that her warmth had a calming influence on the most fractious patient.

He felt an unaccustomed twinge of guilt as he reflected on the way he'd treated her since she'd arrived in the department.

'I took you along because I thought you might learn something and because every A and E doctor should have an idea of what the paramedics deal with on a daily basis.' He saw her soft lips part and was suddenly glad that he was sitting behind the desk. At least she wouldn't be aware of the effect she had on him. 'You were there as an observer. I had no expectations of you as a doctor.'

She stood in silence, watching him warily. She was obviously still expecting an explosion. 'I shouldn't have reacted like that, but I just wasn't prepared for how scary it would be, dealing with a patient at the scene of the accident. I'm used to having masses of medical back-up.'

She obviously felt she'd let herself down badly, which wasn't true at all. He'd seen doctors with many more years' experience than her suddenly freeze at the scene of a serious accident.

It was something to do with the almost overwhelming sense of responsibility that came with being first on the scene.

'Just stick to A and E and don't become a paramedic,' he suggested dryly, and then turned back to his computer, hoping that she'd take the hint and leave him alone.

She didn't. Instead, she took a deep breath, steeling herself to ask the question that had clearly been worrying her. 'You said I ought to be a GP or go back to paediatrics. Do you still think I'll make a bad A and E doctor?'

He felt another twinge of guilt. It was his fault that she was asking the question.

'No. You're a good A and E doctor.'

Surprisingly good.

'But you said—'

'I know what I said. I was angry with you.'

His blunt admission didn't evoke the response he expected. Instead of signs of guilt, she looked confused and taken aback. As if he had no right to be angry.

He had to hand it to her, she was an excellent actress.

She was starting to make *him* feel guilty.

Her blue eyes were suddenly huge and she looked more like a little girl than a fully qualified doctor. 'Why were you angry with me? Because of our...relationship?' She stumbled over the word, looking bemused, and Jago's lean hands curled into fists.

'I thought I had already made it clear that the past is history.'

'But it isn't, is it, Jago? It's there between us the whole time.'

'Let's just say that I have a long memory for certain events.' His tone lethally smooth, he leaned back in his chair and surveyed her with the cool intent of a predator poised for the kill. It really was time for her to drop the innocent act. At least then they'd both know where they stood.

'It must have been extremely challenging for you to keep two men running at the same time with such a limited amount of experience on your part. You must have been very nervous that one of us would find out about the other, and yet it never showed,' he mused, his dark eyes resting on her soft mouth. 'I'm filled with admiration as to how you managed it so skilfully. Tell me, Katy, did you tell him that you loved him, too?'

The air around them throbbed and she stood, frozen to the spot, staring at him with a blank expression.

'I really have no idea what you're talking about.'

She was incredibly beautiful and incredibly dignified. If he hadn't seen the evidence with his own eyes it would have been so easy to believe in her innocence.

'Let's just say that when I enjoy a relationship with a woman, my absolute minimum requirement is fidelity,' he informed her, wondering how she'd cope with being forced to confront her sins. Because he'd made up his mind that she was going to confront them. 'Foolishly, I assumed that as I was your first lover, I didn't need to explain that fact.'

She was still staring at him. 'I still don't know what you mean.'

His gaze hardened. 'I mean that, having been introduced to the joys of sex, you then couldn't wait to spread your wings and sample variety. So tell me, *querida*, was it different with him? Was it worth it?'

She looked startled at his words, hot colour touching her beautiful heart-shaped face, and he was reminded of just how shy she'd been about sex. The product of strict parents and a single-sex school, until she'd met him she'd had virtually no experience of men. He gritted his teeth. Something she'd corrected as quickly as possible.

'Are you saying what I think you're saying? You think that I—' She broke off, her colour deepening, and he gave a wry smile.

'Perhaps you should drop the innocent virgin act now,' he advised. 'I think we've both moved beyond that.'

The colour drained out of her face and she swayed slightly. He felt a flash of concern and then reminded himself that he was dealing with a woman who could sleep with two men at the same time without displaying the slightest flicker of conscience. Now she'd finally been found out he fully expected her to seek refuge in that most female of pastimes. Tears.

'Is that why you left without even a word? Because you believed I was having an affair with someone else?' Her tone was flat and lifeless, her normally sparkly blue eyes dulled with shock and distaste. 'Couldn't you have at least have asked me about it?'

He shrugged a broad shoulder dismissively, his expression sardonic. 'I didn't need to. I had all the evidence I needed. An encounter between us would have been—' He broke off, remembering the searing anger and hurt that he'd felt on discovering her duplicity. His mouth tightened. 'Let's just say that I felt it would be better for both of us if we had no more contact.'

'Evidence?' Her voice was croaky, like someone who hadn't drunk for a week. 'This evidence—who gave it to you?'

He frowned. Surely she should have been asking what

the evidence was? Or was she trying to cover her tracks? 'I don't see the relevance—'

'It was my father, wasn't it?'

So she'd known all along that her father had had incriminating photographs.

'Don't blame him. For once your father was acting honourably. He thought I should know the truth.'

Especially given that ten minutes earlier he had announced his intention of marrying Katy.

Thanks to her father, he'd had a very narrow escape. He owed him a debt.

'Honourably?' Her voice shook and she sank onto the nearest chair, her breathing shallow. She looked terrible. Her cheeks were pale and her slim fingers shook as they clutched the seat of the chair. 'My father has never behaved honourably in his life. He sees what he wants and he goes for it, no matter what obstacles stand in his way. No doubt he manipulated you the same way he manipulates everyone.'

Jago frowned, disconcerted by her unexpected reaction. He'd expected hysterics and denials about the affair. Instead, they seemed to be having a conversation about her father. 'What are you suggesting?'

Katy lifted her head, her eyes dull. 'Show me the photographs.' Her chest rose and fell and she appeared to be struggling to breathe. 'I want to see those photographs. Do you still have them?'

Slight colour touched his cheekbones. 'I don't understand what purpose it would serve—'

'Show me!'

After only the briefest hesitation he reached into his desk and withdrew a large envelope, thoroughly discomfited by the fact that he still had the photographs to hand. It raised questions that he'd never wanted to address before.

But Katy didn't ask questions. She didn't even seem to

find it strange that he had the photographs in his desk eleven years later.

She just ripped at the envelope with shaking hands and emptied the contents onto the desk.

As the glossy prints emerged from the envelope, Jago felt the tension rise in his body. His lean hands fisted and he felt the same sickness he'd felt when he'd first seen them. 'I warn you—they're very revealing.'

She gave an uneven laugh. 'I'm sure they are.' She lifted the photographs, suddenly in possession of an icy control that he'd never seen before.

He frowned slightly, puzzled by her reaction. She certainly wasn't behaving like a woman with a guilty conscience.

As her eyes dropped to the first photograph he averted his eyes. He still wasn't able to look at pictures of her entwined so intimately with another man without wanting to commit grievous bodily harm. *Why the hell had he kept them?* He should have burned them years ago.

She flicked steadily through the pictures, her beautiful face blank.

Then finally she dropped the last one on the pile and lifted her eyes to his. 'I always wondered what made you leave.' Her tone was flat and suddenly all his senses were on alert. Alarm bells were ringing but he didn't know why. She lifted her chin, her eyes glistening with unshed tears. 'You didn't think to ask me about them?'

He was watching her warily now, totally confused by her reaction. Instead of guilt and apology, her blue eyes were full of hurt and accusation.

And disappointment.

Was he missing something here?

'They appear to speak for themselves,' he observed, and she nodded slowly.

'But not when you look at all the facts together.' She turned away from him and walked over to the window, staring out across the courtyard. 'I always wondered what my father said to make you walk away. I knew it had to have been him that ended our relationship. Nothing else made sense.'

Jago was suddenly very still. 'Your father had nothing to do with it. It was my choice to walk away—'

'Yes. You were to blame too, for believing him.' She turned to face him and her eyes were sad. 'He played you like a master, Jago. He did what he does with everyone. He looked for your weakness and then he moved in for the kill.'

Disconcerted and not used to the feeling, Jago stiffened. 'And what was my weakness?'

'Your pride,' she said simply. 'You are, by nature, proud and possessive and my father knew that the one thing that would drive you away from me was finding me with another man. So he made it happen.'

There was an uncomfortable silence while Jago digested her words. 'You're saying that he somehow manufactured these photographs?' He waved a lean brown hand across his desk. 'That they aren't really you?'

'Oh, yes, they're me.' Katy walked back to the desk and picked up the photograph at the top of the pack. 'Good, aren't they? They were taken in a studio in North London when I was modelling. One of the teenage mags wanted some shots to illustrate an article they were doing on safe sex. Aiden and I were supposed to look as though we were in love. Funnily enough, I was more relaxed than I would normally have been because I *was* in love.' Her eyes lifted to his and there was more than a hint of accusation in her clear blue gaze. 'I was in love with *you*, Jago.'

Modelling photographs?

Jago was struggling hard to get a grip on the facts. It hadn't even occurred to him that the photos could have been part of her modelling life.

No. They couldn't be.

Shielding his emotions from her, he glanced at the one on the top of the pile, noticing for the first time all the hallmarks of a professional photographer.

Feeling as though he'd just taken a cold shower, he suppressed a groan. How had he managed to miss that possibility? But he knew the answer, of course. He'd been so furiously angry at what he'd seen as her betrayal that he'd reacted with raw, naked emotion. Had he employed some of the intellect in his possession he might have reached a different conclusion.

But Katy's father had been completely correct in his reading of his character. He'd gambled on the fact that Jago's Spanish pride would prevent him from wanting to contact her again. And the gamble had paid off. He'd walked into the sunset and left her.

He stilled, unable to grasp the fact that he could have made such a colossal misjudgement. 'You never slept with him?'

'No. He's also gay.'

Her tone was flat and Jago tensed, struggling with the appalling reality of having been thoroughly manipulated. 'I thought—'

'I can see what you thought. Please, don't spell it out any further. I find your suppositions totally offensive.' She gathered up the photographs and he reached out and grabbed her wrist, preventing her from leaving.

'Wait.' His fingers tightened. 'If you suspected that your father was responsible, why didn't you come after me?'

She looked at him sadly. 'Because I believed in you. I never knew what made you leave, but I guessed that my father was behind it and for months I held onto this childish dream that our love would prove stronger than my father had anticipated and that you'd come back and at least talk to me. But you never did.'

He flinched at that but his fingers tightened on her wrists.

He needed answers. 'Why would your father do that to you? *To us*?'

'Surely that's obvious. He didn't want us together.' She lifted her eyes to his. 'He found out and he wanted to end it so he bided his time until he found the most effective way. I warned you that we should keep our relationship a secret, but you insisted that you wouldn't creep around.'

Jago's broad shoulders tensed. 'I wasn't afraid of your father.'

'No,' she said quietly. 'But I was. And I was the one left to deal with him after you walked off, Jago. My father didn't know that you had no intention of committing to anyone. For some unfathomable reason he thought you were serious about me and that was the last thing he wanted.'

Jago almost groaned aloud. He *had* been serious.

And he'd made the fatal mistake of telling her father.

Understanding just what had caused her father to take such dramatic steps, Jago ran a hand over his face, lost for words for the first time in his life.

Katy watched him for a long moment and then, with a final pitying look, she tugged her wrist away from his grip, picked up the photographs and left the room without a backward glance.

'Oh, my God.' Libby stared at the photographs in horror. 'Dad gave him these? Well, no wonder the guy walked out. They're very incriminating.'

'I can't believe you just said that!' Katy stared at her in disbelief. 'You're supposed to be on my side.'

'Oh, come on, Katy!' Libby held one of the photographs up and shook her head. 'For crying out loud, you're naked in bed with a man and you're laughing.'

'So? I always liked Aiden,' Katy mumbled, and Libby shook her head.

'Sweetheart, I'm always on your side, you know that,

but for a man as fiercely proud as Jago, these would have seemed like the ultimate insult to his manhood. It's the male ego thing. Can't you see that?' She narrowed her eyes. 'I must admit they're bloody good. You look stunning in this one.'

Katy ignored her. 'But I wouldn't *do* a thing like that. *He should have known* I wouldn't do a thing like that. Instead, he assumed I went from virgin to slut faster than you could say broken heart.'

'I know, and deep down I suspect Jago knows, but love must have clouded his judgement.'

Katy stiffened. She was singularly unimpressed by Jago's judgement. Or rather lack of it. 'We both know that Jago never loved me.'

If he'd loved her, he wouldn't have been so quick to believe the worst of her.

'I certainly didn't think he did,' Libby mused, still leafing through the photographs, 'but now I'm changing my mind.'

'Based on what?'

'Think about it. Think about the way he's been behaving since you walked back into his life—or rather since you arrived on a stretcher. He is *seriously* bothered by you. Also, we both know that Jago is Mr Super-Bright. Nothing gets past him in the intellectual stakes, which can only mean one thing...'

Katy stared at her stupidly and Libby rolled her eyes and dropped the offending photographs on the table.

'He was so blinded by love that he didn't bother examining the facts. His reactions were totally emotional, which was what Dad was banking on when he set it all up.'

'You're being ridiculous,' Katy said. 'Jago couldn't have been in love with me.'

'Why?'

'Well for a start because he never mentioned it,' Katy said caustically, and Libby rolled her eyes to the ceiling.

'So? You're twenty-nine, Katy. When are you going to realise that not everyone is as honest and straightforward as you are? I suspect Jago had never said those three little words in his life before. You'd only been together for a month and you were only eighteen. Maybe if you'd had longer—'

'Well, we didn't,' Katy said flatly, 'and it's history now.'

Libby put the photographs on the table. 'I'd be very surprised if it's history.'

'Meaning?'

'A man like Jago isn't going to let it end there.' Libby's eyes narrowed thoughtfully and the hint of a smile touched her soft mouth. 'And if I were Dad, I'd be shivering in my bed.'

'Yes, well, we both know that nothing disturbs our father's sleep,' Katy said bitterly, not wanting to think about how his interference had affected her life. She didn't know who angered her more. Her father for inventing his lies or Jago for believing them.

And he still didn't know the whole story.

Libby looked at her. 'What if he wants you back now he knows the truth? At the very least he's going to want to talk to you again.'

'There's nothing to talk about,' Katy said flatly. 'It was eleven years ago and in two months' time I'm marrying Freddie. Jago Rodriguez is nothing but a painful part of my past. I know that Dad was responsible, but Jago should have believed in me, Libby. He didn't trust me and I can't be with a man who doesn't trust me.'

'Jago, can you concentrate?'

Jago shook himself and stared at Charlotte. 'Did you say something?'

'Yes.' She put her hands on her hips, her expression frustrated. 'I've been talking to you for the past five minutes and you haven't been listening to a word I've been saying. What's the matter with you?'

'Nothing.' Jago's insides were raw.

After Katy had walked away from him the day before, he'd spent a sleepless night coming to terms with the fact that he'd been successfully manipulated by a master.

He'd always known that Sir Charles Westerling was utterly ruthless, but when that ruthlessness had been turned on him, he hadn't spotted it.

He was also extremely disturbed by Katy's quiet statement that she'd been the one left to deal with her father.

What exactly had she had to deal with?

Had her father been violent?

He was suddenly forced to face the uncomfortable truth that he'd misjudged her appallingly and at the moment he had absolutely no idea how to go about making amends.

He couldn't believe that he'd been so quick to pass judgement on her. Hadn't he seen with his own eyes how shy she was? For goodness' sake, it had taken him *weeks* before he'd even attempted to take things further than a kiss. How could he have believed that she would have been so uninhibited as to dive into another man's bed so quickly?

And she'd loved him. He gritted his teeth. She'd told him so again last night.

She'd loved him with an uncritical devotion that had given him a bigger high than the most lucrative deal he'd ever closed on the stock market.

And he'd managed to kill that love.

'I don't know who's made you angry, but I feel sorry for him,' Charlotte announced, giving up on communication and pushing a set of X-rays in his hands. 'When you've finished plotting revenge, can you check those for me, please? The lady is waiting in cubicle 3.'

Plotting revenge?

He wasn't plotting revenge, there would be time enough to deal with her father later. At the moment he was using every ounce of intelligence at his disposal to try and work out how to manoeuvre his way back into Katy's good books.

And it was going to be tough.

Pulling himself together, he checked the X-ray, reassured the patient and then prowled through A and E, looking for Katy.

She was working in the paediatric area, seeing a child who had fallen awkwardly on a bouncy castle.

The mother was a bag of nerves and the child was cranky and irritable.

Unobserved, he stood in the doorway watching Katy, noticing the way her eyes softened as she spoke to the child and the way she reacted so sympathetically to the mother's endless questions and worries.

Everything about Katy was gentle and giving. She opened windows to let wasps out and lifted spiders out of the bath instead of turning on the taps like most other people. How could he ever have thought she'd have betrayed him with another man?

He watched as she soothed the child and examined the arm, her lower lip caught between her teeth as she ran through the possibilities in her mind.

She was an incredibly thorough doctor.

And he'd treated her shockingly.

'I think she might have fractured a bone, Mrs Hancock,' she said finally. 'She's very tender just here and there's some swelling. I'd like to send her for some X-rays so that I can have a proper look.'

The mother looked guilty. 'It was such a busy party—I didn't even see her fall. I just heard her screaming.'

'How awful for you.' Katy sympathised immediately, her manner completely non-judgmental. 'Try not to blame yourself. These things happen with small children. You can't be everywhere all the time.'

She reached for a form, scribbled on it and handed it to

the mother, the lights catching her blonde hair and making it gleam. 'If you follow the yellow line, that takes you straight to X-Ray. Come back here afterwards and I'll look at the films.'

Jago felt something burn deep inside him.

He still wanted her.

He didn't deserve her but he still wanted her, and all his instincts told him that part of her still wanted him, too. He didn't believe for a moment that she was in love with her fiancé.

If she *had* been, he told himself that he'd have walked away without bothering her, but he'd seen something in her eyes when she'd looked at him.

He'd seen the same hunger that he felt when he was confronted by her every day.

No matter how badly he'd hurt her, physically at least, she still wanted him.

And he intended to use that to his advantage.

Katy finished filling out the notes and then glanced up, the colour fading from her cheeks as she saw Jago watching her.

Her stomach did a somersault.

'Did you need me for something?'

His gaze never flickered from hers. 'We have things to talk about.'

Just as Libby had predicted, he wasn't prepared to leave things as they were.

She straightened. 'We have absolutely nothing to talk about, Jago.'

'I disagree.'

Her eyes slid self-consciously around her, checking that no one was within earshot. 'It's all history, Jago. In the past. Finished.'

'We both know it's far from finished,' he said smoothly, and she tensed.

Surely he wasn't suggesting…?

Just in case he was, she thought she'd better set him straight. 'Jago, you thought I'd given my…' She glanced furtively around again and lowered her voice to little more than a whisper. 'Given my virginity to you and then slept with another man at the same time.' She brushed a strand of hair away from her eyes with shaking fingers, totally unable to comprehend that he'd had such a low opinion of her. 'You obviously didn't know me at all.'

His wide shoulders stiffened defensively. 'I thought I did but all the evidence pointed to the contrary. Surely you can see that.'

She shook her head. 'Jago, I couldn't ever be with a man who believed I was capable of that. I don't know what sort of women you mix with normally but if that's the sort of behaviour that you've come to expect then I feel sorry for you.'

Jago compressed his mouth. 'It does happen.'

She shook her head in disbelief. 'But not with me. I don't *do* things like that,' she said, hating the fact that there was a quiver in her voice. She wanted so badly to match his cool indifference. 'You didn't even have the decency to ask me about it.'

'My only defence is that my pride was very hurt.' He lifted his dark head and looked at her steadily. 'After I left, why didn't you try and contact me? To explain?'

She gaped at him. 'Are you really trying to suggest that any of this is my fault? *You left*—and you didn't even do me the courtesy of telling me you were going, let alone give me the reason for your sudden departure. I was so naïve that I actually believed that you'd come back. That there was nothing on earth that could keep us apart.' She saw him flinch slightly and felt the anger burn inside her. 'But you didn't and I had no idea how to find you. All I knew was that you no longer worked for my father's company. Even when I discovered that I was—'

She caught herself in time and broke off, heart thumping, horrified by what she'd so nearly revealed.

There was a pulsing silence.

'What did you discover, Katy?' He was suddenly incredibly still and his dark eyes were watchful.

'Nothing.' Her voice was a strangled croak and he muttered something in Spanish and moved towards her.

But whatever he'd intended to say, the opportunity was lost as the mother and toddler returned with their X-rays.

Filled with relief at the reprieve, Katy checked them carefully, aware that he was standing close behind her, feeling his warm breath on the back of her neck.

'She's fractured her radius.' Trying to ignore the tense atmosphere, Katy squinted at the X-ray, visually tracing the cortex of each bone as she'd been taught, looking for irregularities. 'There's a slight displacement,' she murmured, 'but that shouldn't matter in a child this young so I'll just give her painkillers and immobilise it in a cast.'

Jago's eyes flickered to the X-rays. 'Have you checked for a second fracture?'

Katy frowned. Was he still trying to catch her out?

'Yes.'

'So what makes you so smart, Dr Westerling,' he muttered under his breath, and she gave a slow smile, ridiculously pleased by the veiled praise.

'I worked in paediatrics,' she reminded him lightly, tugging the X-ray out of the light-box and returning it to the folder.

From a professional point of view, working with him was definitely getting easier. He no longer made her feel as though she should be back in medical school.

Unfortunately their personal relationship was much more complicated.

Katy discussed the management of the fracture with the mother, all the time aware that Jago was standing there, biding his time.

Suddenly she felt hideously nervous and she was desperately searching for an excuse to escape from him when Charlotte hurried down with the news that Ambulance Control had rung to say that they were bringing in a nasty head injury.

With a look of savage frustration on his lean, handsome face, Jago departed, leaving her in no doubt whatsoever that the subject wasn't closed.

CHAPTER SIX

JAGO rang the bell of the flat with impatient fingers and proceeded to pace up and down like a caged tiger.

Ever since their totally unsatisfactory, interrupted conversation, he'd been filled with a rising tension and foreboding.

What had Katy been about to say when she'd stopped in mid-sentence?

Obviously something that she would rather have kept a secret, he reflected grimly, remembering the sudden pallor of her cheeks.

The door suddenly opened and Libby stood there, her blonde hair tumbling over her shoulders, a defiant gleam appearing in her eyes as she recognised him.

'Yes?' Her tone was decidedly unfriendly and he tensed. He wasn't accustomed to receiving such a complete lack of response from a woman.

Obviously he had some serious fence-mending to do with the sister as well as Katy.

'I need to talk to your sister.'

'She's got a date with Freddie tonight,' Libby announced smoothly. 'He's the man she's marrying in two months' time.'

Seeing that she was about to close the door in his face, Jago planted a powerful hand in the middle and pushed it open.

'She won't be marrying him.'

Given no choice but to let him in, Libby backed away from the door and glared at him. 'It took years for her to recover when you walked out last time,' she said frostily. 'Because of what you did she's avoided men like the plague. Don't think Alex and I are going to stand by and let you do it again.'

'I'm not going to hurt her.' Jago stood still, wondering why he felt the need to explain himself to Katy's sister. He wasn't in the habit of explaining himself to anyone. 'I came to finish a conversation. She finally told me everything this morning.'

Libby's blue eyes were suddenly wary. 'What do you mean, *everything*?'

Pushing away the slight niggle that he wasn't playing fair, Jago took instant advantage. He needed the information. He needed to *know*.

'Everything. I know about the baby.' It was no more than an educated guess but he could see from the look in his eyes that he'd hit the jackpot.

'She told you that?' Libby's eyes narrowed. 'She didn't mention it to me this evening.'

Jago's fabled intellect was working overtime, trying to map out a conversation that would give him the information he needed without revealing that there had been no confession.

'Let's just say we've finally started talking about things we should have talked about a long time ago. It must have been terrible for her.'

'It was terrible for all of us. We thought she was going to die for a while,' Libby said softly, her eyes clouded by unpleasant memories. 'She was devastated when you left, but then to lose the baby was the final straw. And she was *so* ill.'

She *lost* the baby?

His baby?

Stunned by the news, Jago masked his expression, determined to elicit all the facts. 'She was in hospital?'

'Of course.' Libby frowned, as if surprised that he should ask such a strange question. 'It was such a bad fall they were really worried about her.'

Jago was battling with the shock of discovering that Katy had been pregnant when he'd left her and had then lost the baby. He was utterly appalled by the notion that he'd somehow failed to protect her. And confused. How could she have become pregnant?

His hard jaw clenched. Had her father known she was pregnant? And why had she fallen?

His brain was still scanning through a variety of equally distasteful scenarios when the door opened and Katy walked into the room.

Dressed for an evening out, she looked incredibly beautiful in a silky black dress and he felt his body tighten in the most basic of male responses. He adored her curves. Like most men, his preference was for women to be shaped like women rather than sticks, and Katy was every inch a woman. The only thing that was wrong with her appearance was her hair.

His mouth tightened as he saw how carefully she'd styled her hair, twisting it and taming it until it lay subdued on top of her head.

She had fabulous hair. Left loose, it fell like a sleek gold curtain almost to her waist and he'd spent hours smoothing his fingers through it, enjoying its amazing scent and texture. But she'd only ever worn it loose when he'd forced the issue. The rest of the time she'd twisted it into submission on the top of her head.

It was the style she always wore for her parents and he hated it. It was restrained, dignified and repressed. All the things that she thought she ought to be. How many times had he ripped the pins out of her hair when they'd been together?

It was as if she was locking an important part of herself away.

He wondered briefly if her fiancé knew what she was really like underneath that elegant, contained exterior and then almost growled with anger at the thought of another man touching her.

She was his.

She'd always been his.

The thought made him catch his breath.

'Jago!' Her startled gaze slid between him and her sister and Libby pulled an apologetic face and backed towards the kitchen.

'Sorry, he forced his way in.' She glared at Jago and then looked pointedly at her sister. 'I'll be making coffee if you need me.'

'Libby—wait!' Katy's plea was ignored and the kitchen door closed firmly behind Libby.

Jago derived some comfort from the fact that Katy hadn't wanted to be left alone with him.

She didn't trust herself.

It gave him a primitive type of male satisfaction to note the way her soft lips parted and her pupils dilated when she looked at him.

He gave a soft smile and stepped towards her.

Katy's eyes locked on Jago's powerful frame and she felt a rush of panic.

He'd come after her.

And hadn't she guessed that he would? Ever since her thoughtless, unguarded comment spoken in the heat of the moment, she'd known that he wouldn't let it go.

His dark gaze locked on hers with the deadly accuracy of a heat-seeking weapon and she felt something unravel deep within her stomach.

It appalled her that he could still make her feel this way. All right, so he was gorgeous, but he was also the man who'd thought her capable of sleeping with two men at the same time. They clearly didn't share the same moral values. How could she still find him even remotely attractive?

But she did. One look at his hard mouth made her skin tingle and her breasts ache.

She felt *hot* all over.

Shocked by the depth of her reaction, drowning in her elemental response to him, Katy sucked in a breath and tried to apply logic to the situation.

Of course she found him attractive. What woman wouldn't? Jago Rodriguez was as sexy as sin. Her reaction didn't mean anything. It was something she could control.

Furiously denying what she was feeling, she reminded herself that she was marrying Freddie in two months' time, and if a tiny voice pointed out that Jago could arouse a response at a distance of metres that Freddie couldn't match even when they were touching, then she chose to ignore it.

There was no way she'd be so foolish as to resume a relationship with Jago again.

Whatever she felt for him, she couldn't be with a man who didn't trust her. And Jago hadn't trusted her.

Having reminded herself firmly of that fact, she tried to match his attitude of cool indifference. 'What are you doing here?'

'Finishing our conversation.' His eyes rested on her mouth with blatant fascination and then slid down her body, his intense scrutiny making her relieved that she was wearing a very modest silk dress. At least he couldn't *see* what she was feeling.

Or could he?

'The conversation was finished, Jago.'

'I don't think so. We'd just reached the part where you were telling me about the baby.'

She was shaken into silence by his smooth declaration and panic clawed at her stomach. 'I didn't say—'

'It was more what you left unsaid,' he finished softly, stepping closer to her. 'Finish the story, Katy.'

She turned and fled towards her bedroom but he was right behind her, closing the door and isolating them together in the confines of the cosy room. Instantly she realised her mistake.

The large, elegant hallway was impersonal whereas everything about her bedroom was soft and intimate. *Personal.*

The last place in the world she'd have chosen to be alone with Jago.

In the hallway of her apartment she hadn't found him particularly intimidating, but in her bedroom she couldn't help but be aware of his superior height and strength. He dominated the room, overwhelmingly male and unshakably confident. And he was looking for answers.

'When did you find out that you were pregnant?'

'After you left.' What was the point in denying what he clearly knew? She walked over the far end of her bedroom, wondering how a room that she normally regarded as a sanctuary could suddenly seem so claustrophobic.

He frowned. 'You didn't find out until after I left?'

She swallowed. 'I suspected…'

'But you didn't say anything?'

'I panicked.'

'I can imagine.' He ran a hand over his jaw, visibly tense. 'Katy, you told me you were protected.'

His voice was surprisingly gentle and her heart missed several beats. If she was vulnerable to his macho, dominating male side, she was even more vulnerable to his gentle side. She wished he'd kept it hidden.

She felt the colour touch her cheeks. 'There really isn't any reason to talk about this.'

'Your sister clearly blames me for making you pregnant,' he pointed out, and she sat down on the edge of the bed because standing suddenly seemed too much like hard work.

'That's not true. I *told* Libby it was my fault.'

He inhaled sharply. 'I was older than you and more experienced. It was my responsibility but you *definitely* told me you were protected.' He stepped forward and hunkered down next to her, his dark gaze fixed on her pale face, his eyes tormented. 'Have you any idea what it does to me to know that I left you pregnant? You lied to me, *querida*. Why?'

'Because I was eighteen and stupid,' she muttered, her cheeks hot with embarrassment. 'And desperate.'

He frowned with an unusual lack of comprehension. 'Desperate?'

'To go to bed with you.'

She looked away from him, instantly regretting her honesty, but strong fingers caught her chin and forced her to look at him.

Connecting with those stunning dark eyes, she suddenly understood with appalling clarity how she could have made such a serious error of judgement at eighteen. Jago was so staggeringly sexy that exercising common sense would have been as unlikely as a snowstorm in summer.

He said something under his breath in Spanish and then switched to English. 'I can't believe I let that happen,' he muttered, and her eyes slid away from his.

'I've never blamed you.'

'You should have told me you were pregnant.'

'I had no idea where you were,' she pointed out, struggling to control the traitorous reaction of her body. He was so close to her. She curled her fingers into her palms in case she gave in to the temptation to slide them into his silky black hair. 'And, anyway, you'd rejected me.'

He gave an agonised groan. 'Don't remind me. If I'd known...' His face was unusually pale, the skin stretched taut over his cheekbones. 'And then you lost the baby. How did you fall? Tell me what happened.'

Shaken by a question that she hadn't been anticipating, she stared at him. 'How did you know I fell?'

'I'm afraid I took advantage of your sister,' he muttered, and she stood up and moved over to her bedroom window.

He was being too nice to her. The only way she could keep him at a distance was if she reminded herself that he was an uncaring, unfeeling monster who hadn't trusted her, and it was very hard to do that convincingly when he was working overtime on demonstrating his sensitive side.

She desperately wanted him to leave.

Unfortunately Freddie wasn't due for another half-hour so there was no hope of a reprieve from that direction.

'Katy?' Eyes narrowed, Jago rose to his feet in a fluid movement and she stopped to pick up a towelling robe, which lay discarded on the floor, and draped it over the back of a chair.

Anything to avoid that penetrating gaze. He saw too much.

'I tripped—it was just one of those things.'

There was a long silence. 'You *tripped*?'

She licked her lips, hearing the surprise and disbelief in his tone. 'That's right. And now can we change the subject?' She looked at him and managed something resembling a smile. 'As you're always saying, it's history now and I certainly don't blame you for the baby.'

His powerful body radiated tension. 'But you blame me for everything else.'

'You should have trusted me, Jago,' she said simply. 'I was completely in love with you and a man as experienced as you should have seen that I couldn't see straight enough to focus on another man.'

A muscle moved in his cheek and she watched him dealing with the unfamiliar experience of being in the wrong.

For a man with his pride she knew it would be hard and she certainly wasn't expecting an apology. Jago had probably never apologised for anything in his life.

'You have to admit I had reason—'

'You ignored what you knew about me and judged me on the evidence of someone who had every reason to destroy our relationship,' she said quietly, holding onto the fact that he'd behaved with such totally predictable male arrogance. Only by remembering that would she be able to keep him at a distance. 'I still can't quite believe you did that. And now you have to go, Jago. Freddie will be here any minute.'

'Call him and cancel.'

He moved towards her with deliberate intent and she found herself backing against the wall of the bedroom.

'He's booked a table.'

'Cancel.' His eyes dropped to her mouth and she felt her heart rate increase with startling rapidity. 'You're not going to marry him, Katy.'

The atmosphere in the room was suddenly charged with tension and she felt frighteningly out of control.

'I *am*, I'm—'

'Call him and end it. We both know you're not in love with him. So why are you marrying him?'

Because she didn't *want* love.

Jago stepped closer still and she felt sensation knife through her pelvis. She was breathlessly aware of him, of the blue-black stubble on his jaw, of the slumberous dark eyes probing hers with relentless intent, of his wide shoulders blocking her escape.

'You're dating a Brazilian model,' she reminded him desperately, and he gave a groan of denial.

'Not any more.'

Trapped by his ferocious masculinity, she felt the tension in the room rise to an almost unbearable degree.

'End it,' he instructed softly, his eyes dropping to her parted lips and clouding hungrily, 'or stop looking at me like that.'

She couldn't get the air into her lungs. 'I'm not looking at you—'

'Yes, you are.'

Without warning he took her mouth in a kiss so explicit in its intent that her senses went into freefall. With a rough exclamation he hauled her against his powerful body, the sensual onslaught of his kiss creating an excitement so wild that she couldn't help but respond. Fevered by his touch, she kissed him back, locking her arms around his strong neck, feeling the heat of his body pressing through the thin fabric of her dress.

His breathing fractured, he lifted a hand and tugged roughly at her hair, discarding the clips impatiently until it tumbled in a silken mass over his arm and down her back.

With a groan of satisfaction he sank both hands into the soft waves that he'd released, anchoring her head against the relentless onslaught of his skilled mouth.

'I love your hair.' He muttered the words against her mouth, moving his lips over hers, exploring suggestively with his tongue until she went up in flames.

How could she have forgotten what it felt like to kiss Jago?

Instead of pulling away, she pressed herself closer to him, quivering with response as he kissed her senseless.

Her body softened under the hard possession of his mouth, her insides melting as his tongue probed and teased in an erotic reminder of more intimate moments.

'Jago, *please…*' She was out of her mind with excitement, her whole body consumed by a wild hunger that was totally outside her control.

She needed him so badly.

It had been so long.

The hot demands of his mouth intensified and she started to shiver, held in the grip of an electrifying force so powerful that that she thought she might explode.

She felt frantic.

Desperate.

When Jago finally dragged his mouth away from hers, she staggered slightly, grateful that his fingers were gripping her arms so tightly. If they hadn't been, she would undoubtedly have fallen.

Aghast and embarrassed by the uninhibited way she'd responded to him, she freed herself from his grip and backed away, deriving some small satisfaction from the fact that Jago looked as stunned as she felt.

Maybe he wasn't quite as cool and in control as he liked to pretend.

He sucked in his breath and took a step backwards, reaching out to steady himself as he almost tripped over the chair.

His dark eyes burned into hers. 'You *definitely* need to call Freddie.'

With that parting shot he turned and strode out of the room, leaving her staring after him in trembling disbelief, feeling intensely vulnerable.

What had she done?

She'd kissed Jago.

And that hadn't been any old kiss. That kiss had been as close to sex as it was possible to get without removing clothing.

She groaned in mortification. Knowing Jago, he wasn't going to let her forget it. He was self-confident and arrogant enough to have taken that response as a green light. From now on he'd be pursuing her with all the subtlety of a herd bull.

Shocked and confused, she sat on the edge of the bed until the sound of the doorbell disturbed her.

It would be Freddie. What was she going to do?

She stared at the closed door with something close to desperation.

She was engaged to Freddie but she'd kissed Jago. And kissing Jago had exposed her to a level of excitement that she'd denied herself for eleven years. Intense, toe-curling excitement that could so easily become addictive.

Lifting a hand, she touched her lips, still able to feel a slight tingling where he'd plundered her mouth with his.

No one but no one kissed like Jago. Jago had cornered the market in sexual excitement.

Hearing Freddie's voice in the hallway, she closed her eyes, knowing that she needed to make a decision.

Fingers shaking, she stood up just as Freddie tapped on the door and walked in. He stopped in surprise, visibly taken aback by her appearance.

'Goodness, Katherine, what have you done to your hair?' His frown was faintly disapproving. 'The Fletcher-Gibbs are quite formal usually and this evening is very much a business dinner. There'll be clients there. You might want to wear it up.'

Katy blinked, suddenly realising that she'd forgotten to redo her hair after Jago had strode like the conquering male out of her bedroom, having kissed her to the point of total surrender.

She lifted a hand and realised that her long blonde hair, normally fiercely restrained, was flowing loose over her shoulders.

'I—I—' She broke off, suddenly needing to ask him a question. 'Freddie, do you like it like this? If we weren't dining with the Fletcher-Gibbs, would you prefer that I left it down?'

He looked at her with the expression of a man who knew he was on dangerous ground. 'You look lovely,' he said tactfully, 'but generally speaking I prefer it up. It projects the right sort of image, don't you agree?'

And that was what Freddie cared about, of course. Image.

Katy looked at him thoughtfully. Jago didn't prefer it up. Her hair had always driven him wild. But, then, as Libby had pointed out, Freddie wasn't the sort of man to be driven wild by anything except stocks and shares.

And that had been one of the reasons she'd agreed to marry him.

But what was she going to do now?

Could she ever be satisfied with the blandness of Freddie after experiencing the heat and colour of a man like Jago?

CHAPTER SEVEN

JAGO strode through the A and E department the next morning, satisfied that he'd successfully salvaged what could have been a difficult situation.

All right, so he'd made a mistake about Katy, but her response to his kiss had more than convinced him that she'd forgiven him for not trusting her. After the kiss they'd shared the night before he was supremely confident that she would have ended her engagement to Freddie.

Which meant that they could resume their relationship.

And he had every intention of doing exactly that.

He loved her.

He'd always loved her.

Convinced that he had the situation well in hand, it came as an enormous shock to see her clutching a huge hand-tied bouquet of flowers as she walked along the corridor towards him.

Instinct told him that they had to be from Freddie and he tensed in stunned disbelief. What sort of guy sent flowers after he'd been dumped only a few months before the wedding?

Unless she hadn't dumped him.

Maybe his plan wasn't going quite as smoothly as he'd anticipated.

'You didn't do it?' He glowered at her, disconcerted by the feeling that tore through him. The feeling that he only ever seemed to experience when he was around Katy. 'I can't believe you still intend to marry that man. How can you marry him after the way you kissed me last night?'

'*You* kissed *me*, Jago,' she pointed out calmly. 'And please don't criticise Freddie. He's romantic and kind.'

Romantic?

She thought Freddie was romantic?

He stiffened, offended by the implication that he was somehow lacking in that direction. 'You don't think I'm romantic?'

'You?' She looked startled at the question, as if the thought genuinely hadn't occurred to her before. 'You don't have a romantic bone in your body, Jago.'

Rocked from his unshakable conviction that he was the only man she'd ever wanted, Jago was completely wrong-footed. 'This isn't the place to have the type of conversation we need. I'm taking you to dinner tonight. I'll pick you up at eight-thirty. We can talk then.'

'And you think you're romantic?' She shook her head, her expression sympathetic and slightly amused. 'Sorry. I'm already going out.'

With Freddie no doubt.

His lean hands curled into fists. 'You still want me, Katy, and I want you.'

Having laid most of his cards on the table, Jago watched her warily, trying to gauge her reaction. Normally he prided himself in his ability to understand and outsmart the most devious member of her sex, but Katy didn't play any of the games that women normally played. Whatever reaction he was expecting to that declaration, it wasn't the one he received.

Instead of falling into his arms and treating his announcement with the misty-eyed delight that he'd expected, she merely looked at him, visibly unenthusiastic at the prospect of resuming their relationship.

Uncomfortably aware that nothing was going according to plan, Jago suddenly found himself in the novel position of not knowing how to handle a woman. After that kiss he'd assumed that they'd be resuming their relationship as soon as she'd ended her engagement to Freddie. But there was something disturbingly discouraging about the expression in her blue gaze.

'Up until twenty-four hours ago you believed me capable of sleeping with another man, even though I'd told you that I was in love with you.' Her tone was cool and controlled. 'You told me yesterday that your barest minimum requirement in a relationship is fidelity. Well, mine is trust, Jago. I absolutely cannot be with a man who doesn't trust me.'

Jago sucked in a breath. 'I already explained what happened.'

'And that's supposed to make it OK?' Her voice shook slightly and he realised that she wasn't quite as cool as she was making out. 'You didn't trust me, Jago. I doubt that you've ever trusted anyone. You move on before you can get close to a woman.'

Thoroughly discomfited by her blunt appraisal, he took refuge in attack. 'You still want me, Katy. Do you think I didn't feel it when we kissed last night?'

'A relationship has to be based on more than kissing. I'm not interested, Jago.' Her grip on the flowers tightened. 'We might have to work together, but I don't want anything else.'

And with that parting shot she walked off, leaving him to come to terms with the fact that for the first time in his thirty-five years, a woman had chosen to walk away from him.

He wanted her back.

Katy stuffed the flowers in water so that they didn't die before the end of her shift and slipped the card into her pocket with shaking fingers.

She wondered what Jago would have said had he known that they weren't from Freddie at all but from Alex, whom she'd spoken to on the phone the night before. And it was Alex she was having dinner with. Alex and Libby.

In fact, his hasty assumption that she hadn't broken up

with Freddie was yet another indication of Jago's jaundiced view of her sex. He was assuming that, despite the kiss they'd shared, she was still going ahead and marrying another man.

She wondered what had happened in his life that made him so cynical about women.

It showed that he still knew very little about her. She would never do a thing like that.

She would never kiss one man and then marry another.

And that was the reason she'd ended her engagement to Freddie the evening before.

She felt slightly guilty about not telling Jago but she hadn't actually lied, she reassured herself. She just hadn't told the whole truth.

And why should she?

Jago didn't love her. All he wanted was a physical affair and she knew that pursuing a relationship with Jago would be a quick route to another broken heart. They just didn't want the same things in life. So surely she was right to protect herself?

She walked out of the staffroom, reflecting that breaking up with Freddie had been surprisingly painless. Even though initially he'd seemed a little startled by her announcement that she couldn't marry him, he'd accepted it with a readiness that suggested that he'd been having second thoughts about the wedding himself. She just wished that telling her parents would prove as easy.

She needed to pick the right time to do it but it had to be soon, otherwise they'd hear from other sources.

The morning was incredibly busy but she successfully avoided Jago until lunchtime when the doors to the ambulance bay crashed open and the paramedics rushed in with a small girl on the stretcher.

'This is Molly Churchman. She's two years old and she fell out of the bedroom window,' the paramedic told them, his expression tense and anxious. 'Bedroom on the first floor—the mother is hysterical.'

Jago reached for the oxygen mask and positioned it carefully over the child's mouth and nose. He watched carefully, nodding with satisfaction as he saw the mask fog.

'Her airway is patent and she's breathing by herself,' he growled. 'I want two lines in and I need an estimation of her weight.'

Katy wondered whether it was the sick child or their earlier confrontation that was responsible for the grim expression on his handsome face and the tension in his broad shoulders.

It was probably the child, she decided. Their relationship couldn't possibly be that important to him.

Charlotte looked up. 'I asked the mother about her weight but she was too upset to give me a lucid answer.'

'In that case, use the Oakley Paediatric Resuscitation chart on the wall,' Jago instructed, and one of the other nurses hurried to do that while he carried on assessing the child. 'Cervical spine injury is rare in a child of this age but we'll keep the spine immobilised until we've ruled it out.'

There was a flurry of action and Annie came back from examining the chart on the wall. 'Estimated weight is about 12 kilograms.'

'Right. Charlotte, make a note of that. Annie, go back to the mother,' Jago ordered, 'find out if the child cried immediately—I need to know whether she was unconscious for any time. And get me details of allergies, medications, past medical history and when she last ate or drank. And try and get a more precise account of the accident. What surface she landed on, how she was lying—that sort of thing.'

Annie hurried off to do as he'd instructed and Jago spoke quietly to the little girl, reassuring her in a gentle voice as he worked.

Charlotte was visibly upset as she undressed the child so that they could make a more accurate assessment of her injuries.

'She's so tiny. That poor mother.'

'Lose the emotion,' Jago said harshly. 'We've got a job to do. Finish undressing her and get some overhead heaters and warming blankets—a fall in body temperature causes a rise in oxygen consumption.'

Charlotte swallowed and looked at him, startled by the sharp reprimand.

Katy felt a flash of empathy for her colleague but she knew that Jago was right.

It wouldn't help the child if they let emotions get in the way of their work. The child needed them to be professional.

But there was no doubt that Jago was unusually tense.

They removed all her clothes and then covered her in warm blankets and adjusted the heaters so that she wouldn't become cold.

With the minimum of fuss, Katy found a vein and slipped in the cannula.

'Her blood pressure is slightly down,' one of the nurses said, 'but not dramatically.'

'Check her capillary refill time,' Jago ordered, and Katy finished taping the first IV in place and glanced up at him.

'Is that significant?'

He gave a brief nod. 'A child can suffer considerable blood loss without a significant change to the vital signs,' he told her, his eyes fixed on her fingers as she searched for another vein. 'When we diagnose shock in children we rely on other signs, like capillary refill time, the appearance of the skin, the temperature of the extremities.'

'Based on those criteria, this child is in shock,' Katy murmured, pausing as she located what felt like a vein.

Without hesitating, she inserted the cannula smoothly and watched as the blood flowed backwards.

'Both lines are in,' she said quickly, relieved that she'd managed what had proved to be a difficult task. Finding veins in a child that small was difficult at the best of times and sometimes they had to give an infusion directly into the bone.

The child had barely protested, which was another indication of how ill she was.

'That was a tricky job.' Jago's voice was gruff. 'Well done.'

For a brief moment their eyes met and he gave a slight smile. The tension in the room seemed to ease slightly but there was a hint of challenge in that smile that made Katy breathless.

The subject of their relationship was obviously far from closed.

She picked up a selection of blood bottles. 'I'll take bloods for group and cross-matching, blood-glucose estimation and request a full blood count and biochemistry. Anything else?'

Jago shook his head. 'No, but we need to get her some pain control.'

'Her skin is very cold and clammy and her capillary refill time is prolonged,' Charlotte said quietly, and Katy bit her lip as she took the bloods and administered the pain relief that Jago had ordered.

'She's very lethargic,' Jago murmured, his eyes never leaving the child as he worked. 'She's showing all the features of class III shock. I want to give her 20 milligrams of crystalloid per kilogram. Do the calculation, Katy.'

Katy did as he ordered and warmed the fluid before injecting it into the child's vein.

Jago carried on examining the limp, unresponsive body of the toddler. 'She's bleeding from somewhere and we need to find out where. Check her pulse and blood pressure again,' he ordered, glancing at Charlotte as he spoke. 'I've got a bad feeling about this. Bleep the surgeons and get me some blood up here fast. If her vital signs don't improve in the next few minutes I'm going to transfuse her. Can we get a nasogastric tube down, please? And I want X-rays of her chest and pelvis.'

Katy looked at the tiny body on the trolley and, despite Jago's warnings about becoming emotional, she felt a lump in her throat.

The little girl was so tiny and helpless. No wonder the mother was hysterical. She would have been hysterical if it had been her child who was lying there injured.

They had to save the child. They just couldn't let her die.

A niggling suspicion entered her head and she opened her mouth to speak and then closed it again.

'What?' Jago's tone was sharp. 'You were going to say something.'

Katy hesitated. 'I was wondering whether it could be her spleen,' she said quietly, 'but there's no clinical reason to imagine that it could be. Just a gut feeling.'

'Never dismiss gut feelings.' Jago looked at her and then returned his attention to the child, his expression thoughtful. 'It would explain the degree of shock in the absence of visible injury.'

Annie returned, having interviewed the mother in more depth, and she gave a full report to Jago who had examined the X-rays and now had his eyes fixed on the abdominal ultrasound.

'She's bleeding into her abdomen,' he muttered, and Carl, one of the other junior doctors, looked at him questioningly.

'But her abdominal wall is barely bruised.'

'That isn't a reliable sign in children.' Jago didn't look up. 'She's showing signs of abdominal injury. I think Katy is probably right. It's her spleen.'

Carl rubbed a hand over the back of his neck. 'So we need to get her to Theatre urgently?'

'Not necessarily.' Jago shook his head. 'We tend to avoid surgery and adopt a conservative approach where possible. The spleen is the most commonly injured organ following blunt trauma to the abdomen, then the liver and kidneys.'

'If it is her spleen, will they try leaving it to heal by itself?' Katy frowned, racking her brains to recall the detail of something she'd seen in a medical journal. 'Didn't I read something recently that suggested that removing the spleen can result in significant long-term health problems?'

'That's right.' Jago nodded. 'It's very unusual to remove the spleen these days.'

Charlotte checked the child's vital signs again. 'I think she's improving. That fluid is helping.'

At that moment the doors opened and the surgical team swarmed into Resus.

They conferred with Jago, checked the abdominal ultrasound and examined the child carefully.

'I think you're right,' the consultant said finally, glancing at Jago with a slight smile. 'I'd say she has a small tear in her spleen.'

Jago glanced at Katy and a slight smile touched his firm mouth. 'It was Dr Westerling's diagnosis,' he said softly, and the consultant gave her an approving nod.

'In that case, well done to you, Dr Westerling. We'll get a CT scan and take it from there. If her signs continue to improve, we'll manage it conservatively. Are the parents with her?'

'The mother's in the relatives' room,' Jago said, ripping off his gloves and dropping them in the bin. 'I'm going to speak to her now. Katy, you can come with me as this seems to have turned into your case.'

Warmed by his approval, Katy blushed slightly. Despite his encouraging comments, she was well aware that it was he who had saved the child.

'Do you think she's going to live?' Katy quickened her stride to keep pace with him as he strode out of Resus and made for the relatives' room. She'd never been assigned the task of talking to relatives before, and was relieved that he was there to do it with her.

Jago pulled a face. 'Because children are so small, a fall like that can cause multisystem injury. You have to assume that they have multiple injuries until proved otherwise. If it's just a small tear to her spleen, she should recover fully.'

'You were so calm.'

He cast her a wry smile that was thoroughly unexpected. 'Not that calm.' He paused for a moment, his dark eyes resting on her face. 'I have feelings, too, you know.'

She looked at him, breathless, wondering whether he was just referring to Molly.

'But you don't show them.'

He lifted a broad shoulder in a shrug. 'How would that help the child? The patient needs me to be detached and efficient. Emotion clouds judgement, Katy. Remember that.'

He gave a twisted smile and suddenly she knew what he was thinking.

That emotion had clouded his judgement eleven years ago when he'd seen those photographs.

And in a way, wasn't it the same for her?

She knew that loving Jago was a quick road to heartache but she just couldn't help herself. He was drop-dead gorgeous and seeing him save a child's life with such impressive skill and supreme coolness made her want to surrender to him on the spot.

She studied him helplessly.

Everything about him was just so masculine. From his straight, aristocratic nose and perfect bone structure to the blue-black stubble beginning to show on his hard jaw, he was one hundred per cent red-blooded male and she realised with a sinking heart that she'd never stopped loving him.

Realising that they'd reached the relatives' room, she

jerked her eyes away from his sinfully sexy mouth and tried to concentrate.

'Don't you usually take a nurse with you to do the gentle, caring bit?'

He dealt her a sizzling smile that cranked her pulse rate up still higher. 'Why do you think I've brought you along?'

Without waiting for her reply, he pushed open the door with his shoulder and extended a hand to the woman sitting slumped in one of the armchairs.

'Mrs Churchman? I'm Mr Rodriguez, one of the A and E consultants. This is Dr Westerling. We looked after Molly in the resuscitation room.'

Katy closed the door behind them and went to sit beside the mother, concerned that she looked so distraught. Annie had told them that she hadn't even wanted to see her daughter in the resuscitation room.

'I've killed her. I know I've killed her.'

She started to sob hysterically and Katy glanced at Jago, expecting to see him tense and uncomfortable in the face of such hysterics. Instead, he frowned in concern and hunkered down next to the sobbing woman, taking her hand in his.

'You haven't killed her, Mrs Churchman.' His voice was warm and firm. 'She had a bad fall and she is suffering from some internal injuries but she is doing very well at the moment. We've transferred her to the children's surgical ward for some more tests and observation.'

The young mother looked at him, her chest jerking as she tried to hold back the sobs. 'She climbed out of the window.'

Jago nodded. 'So I understand.'

'I didn't even know she could reach the window,' Mrs Churchman whispered, horror in her voice as she related the tale. 'She pulled up a chair and climbed onto the window-sill. I was changing her bed at the time and I'd only nipped out for a moment to fetch a clean sheet. I must have been out of the room for less than thirty seconds, no more.'

She gave another sob and Katy reached for a box of tissues. 'Being a parent is the most difficult, responsible job in the world,' she said quietly. 'What Molly needs now is not for you to feel guilty but for you to be there for her. She needs her mother.'

Mrs Churchman blew her nose and nodded. 'You're right, I know you're right. But seeing her lying there as if she was dead just upset me so much.'

Jago frowned. 'She isn't dead, Mrs Churchman.' He went on to outline Molly's injuries and treatment in a cool, factual way and eventually the young mother seemed to gain some measure of control.

'Can I see her now?'

Katy nodded. 'When you're ready, one of the nurses will take you to the children's ward and you'll be able to stay with her. Is there anyone you'd like us to call to be with you?'

Mrs Churchman shook her head and reached for her bag. 'No. Her father is away on business and I don't want to worry my parents with it. I'll be fine now.'

Looking at her pale face, Katy wasn't so sure and she made a mental note to check on her later.

Leaving Mrs Churchman to gather her belongings together, they left the room and Katy arranged for a nurse to escort her to the ward.

'I'm glad you were there,' Jago said dryly as they walked back towards the main area of the A and E department. 'Dealing with hysterical females is not my strong point.'

She smiled at him. 'I thought you were brilliant.'

'Well, thank you,' Jago drawled softly, pausing as one of the other casualty officers waylaid him to ask his opinion on an X-ray.

Jago took the film in question and pushed it into the

nearest light-box, his gaze fixed on the X-ray in front of him. 'There's a hairline fracture on the anterior view.'

The doctor muttered his thanks, looked slightly embarrassed that he hadn't spotted it himself and then hurried off to manage the patient accordingly.

Katy staring at Jago with a mixture of admiration and frustration. 'You never miss anything, do you? Has anyone ever told you that you set impossibly high standards?'

'This is an A and E department,' Jago reminded her with a careless lift of his broad shoulders. 'How can standards ever be too high? If we get it wrong, people die. And in this wonderful age of litigation, if we were even remotely to blame, we're sued.'

They walked on down the corridor and Katy bit her lip, knowing that there was some truth in what he said.

People *were* much quicker to apportion blame these days.

'Well, I for one am glad you have high standards. You were great with Molly,' she said softly, and he glanced towards her.

'So were you,' he said equally softly, a wry smile pulling at the corners of his mouth. 'You're a good doctor, Katy. You have good instincts.'

She looked at him and found her gaze trapped by his. The tension pulsed between them and she took a step backwards, stunned by the intensity of the attraction.

Breathing hard she tried to pull herself together.

He hadn't trusted her.

She had to keep reminding herself of that fact.

'I hope Molly will be all right.'

The faint amusement in his dark eyes indicated that he was well aware of her internal struggle. 'She was lucky,' he said smoothly. 'That mother should have had locks on the upstairs windows.' With a last lingering look at her mouth he turned away from her and walked back towards the main area of the A and E department, obviously expecting her to follow. 'She was totally negligent.'

Katy was taken aback by his sharp comment. 'Children move so fast—'

'And it is a mother's job to be one step ahead of them,' he shot back, his expression disapproving. 'A two-year-old girl should *not* be falling out of windows, no matter how hot the weather.'

'Accidents happen,' Katy reminded him gently. 'People make mistakes. You're very judgmental.'

'And you're very forgiving, *querida*,' he observed, stopping dead in his tracks, his dark lashes hiding his expression from her, 'except, it would seem, when I'm the culprit.'

Heat rushed to her face and she bit her lip, flustered by the hint of a smile pulling at the corners of his firm mouth.

'Jago—'

'Tell me, Katy.' He stepped closer to her and lowered his voice. 'How long are you going to keep up this pretence?'

She licked dry lips and then immediately wished she hadn't as his dark eyes lasered in on the gesture with visible hunger. 'What pretence?'

'The pretence that there's nothing between us.' With obvious reluctance his eyes lifted to hers, holding her captive. 'What does a guy have to do to get you to forgive? Send flowers? Beg?'

Her body slowly heated up under his gaze, sexual excitement burning low in her stomach. Why did being close to Jago *always* have this effect on her?

'I—I forgive you,' she stammered, backing away slightly from his powerful presence. 'But it doesn't mean I want a relationship. We're too different, Jago. We want different things.'

He gave a smile that was pure predatory male. 'I don't think so.'

'That's just sex!' She said the words without thinking and then looked round in embarrassment, realising that any of the staff could have been within earshot. Fortunately they weren't. 'You left me, Jago. You left me without a backward glance. Give me one instance that proves that you cared about me and not just the sex.'

'I kept the photographs,' he reminded her simply, a smile of satisfaction appearing in direct response to her shocked expression. 'Think about that, *querida*.'

With that he touched her on the cheek and walked away, leaving her staring after him.

He'd almost told her about the ring.

Jago stared at a conference programme, bombarded by totally alien emotions. He sensed that whatever he said at the moment, it wouldn't be enough. Katy was incurably romantic. As a child she'd played with dolls and dreamed of princes. And none of those dreams had included a prince who left her when the going got tough. It was going to take some very fancy footwork on his part to convince her that he loved her.

He'd always loved her.

And eleven years before she'd been madly in love with him, and he'd killed that love with his lack of trust.

Somehow he had to win that love back.

But how?

Despite her passionate response to his kiss and the fact that her whole body reacted when he walked into the same room as her, Katy wasn't showing any signs of wishing to renew their relationship.

Remembering the way she'd clutched the flowers that morning, his fingers tightened on the programme.

She'd been delighted with them. And she clearly hadn't broken off her engagement to Freddie.

With a muttered curse he ran a hand over the back of his neck, acknowledging with unusual insight that it was

going to take more than an exotic bunch of flowers to re-
deem himself in Katy's eyes.

Thanks to a major overreaction on his part over the photographs, she was now completely convinced that he didn't
possess a sensitive side.

With a groan of frustration he tossed the programme onto
the desk and applied his brain to the intellectual challenge
of how to convince Katy he was as caring as the next guy.

He was absolutely sure about one thing—their relationship was never going to progress unless he got her away
from the hospital and away from Freddie.

With a complete lack of vanity he recognised the fact
that she was marrying Freddie because she was afraid of
the feelings she had for *him*.

Katy was soft-hearted and loving and he'd hurt her
badly. She didn't want to be hurt again and he'd seriously
underestimated her strength of will. Once he'd apologised
for having misjudged her, he'd stood back and waited for
her to fall back into his arms.

But instead she'd walked away and now he found himself in the unique position of having to chase after a woman
he wanted.

He looked at the conference programme again and an
idea suddenly formed in his mind.

He was due to present a paper at a major medical conference in Seville at the end of the week and he'd arranged
to visit his family afterwards.

He had space for one other doctor.

'Have you heard there's a place for a doctor to go to the
conference in Seville at the end of the week? Apparently
Harry was due to go but had to drop out at the last minute.'
Several of the casualty officers were gathered around the
noticeboard in the staffroom when Katy walked in and
pushed her bag in the locker. Her mind was still on the
confrontation she'd had with her parents the night before.

Her mother had been hysterical at the news that the wedding was off and her father had refused to accept that she was no longer marrying Freddie.

All in all it had been an extremely unpleasant evening.

Her colleagues were still looking at the noticeboard and chatting. 'Mr Rodriguez is presenting a paper and he's allowed to take someone with him. If you want to go you have to sign your name and then they're going to put the names in a hat.'

'Very scientific.'

Only half listening to the conversation, Katy checked that her hair was neatly tied back and walked onto the unit without signing her name. She was struggling to cope with Jago in the impersonal atmosphere of the A and E department without subjecting herself to the intimacy of a foreign trip.

As far as she was concerned, one of the others was more than welcome to go.

The waiting room was crowded with people and Katy didn't have time to give the trip another thought until one of her colleagues approached her at lunchtime with a rueful smile.

'Well, you're the lucky one.'

Katy stared at him blankly. 'I am?'

'Your name was pulled out of the hat. You're going to Seville with the boss.'

Katy put her sandwich down untouched. 'That's not possible.'

She hadn't even put her name on the board.

'Finding it hard to believe your luck?' The other doctor grinned at her. 'You shouldn't feel guilty. It was all done fair and square. I was the one who pulled your name out of the hat.'

But her name shouldn't have been *in* the hat.

Totally appalled by the prospect of attending the conference with Jago, Katy got to her feet and knocked the chair over.

'Hey, steady on.' Her colleague looked at her in amusement. 'I know you're excited but you don't want to injure yourself before you go.'

She didn't wait to hear the rest of what he had to say. She needed to see Jago.

He was in his office, working on the computer, and she marched in without knocking.

'How did my name get in that hat, Jago?'

She glared at him angrily, her irritation increasing at his total lack of reaction.

'What hat?'

'Don't pretend you don't know what I'm talking about.' Suddenly aware that they could be overheard, she closed the door firmly and stalked across to his desk. 'I understand my name has been pulled out of the hat to go with you to Seville.'

'Has it?' His voice was a low drawl and he didn't lift his eyes from the spreadsheet he was working on. 'Don't complain. That place was very much in demand.'

'But not by me.' Frustration bubbled up inside her. 'You're not listening to me!'

Finally he looked at her, his gaze cool. If he was playing games then there was certainly no sign of it.

She took a deep breath and tried again. 'I didn't put my name on that list. I don't *want* to go with you to Seville.'

One dark eyebrow lifted. 'It's a first-class meeting with some excellent speakers,' he said calmly. 'You'll find it very informative and useful.'

'I'm sure the meeting will be great. This isn't about the meeting.'

'So what's bothering you?'

He was bothering her. And he knew it.

She licked her lips. 'Jago, I can't go with you.'

He sprawled back in his chair, his expression mocking. 'Am I that dangerous?'

Yes.

He gave a slow smile. 'It doesn't say much for your relationship with Freddie if you can't trust yourself to be alone with me,' he observed softly, and she coloured slightly, uncomfortable with the fact that she hadn't corrected his assumption that her wedding was still going ahead.

Why hadn't she?

Because she'd hoped that his belief that she was still engaged would encourage him to back off.

But she could see from the look in his eyes that he had no intention of backing off. He wanted her and he was going after her with all the ruthless determination that was so much a part of his character.

'Let yourself go, Katy,' he advised. 'Be yourself. Stop trying to be what your parents want you to be.'

Wasn't that what Libby and Alex were always saying?

'I am myself,' she said finally, her mouth dry and her heart pumping hard at the mere thought of being alone on foreign soil with Jago.

'Then, in that case, there isn't a problem, is there?' With a cool smile he reached across his desk and handed her a file. 'The flights and accommodation are all arranged and the programme is in there—you might like to look at it. I'm presenting on the first day but it runs for four days in total.'

Four days in Jago's company?

Her mind numb, she took the file, still wondering how her name had come to be added to the list. Jago hadn't admitted that he'd been responsible but he hadn't exactly denied it either. And the question was academic now. She could hardly refuse to go without drawing attention to herself. The other doctors saw it as a fantastic opportunity to catch up on the latest developments in the field of emergency medicine and if it had just been about the conference she would have been excited, too.

But it wasn't about the conference.

It was about being alone with Jago. Jago, who wanted nothing more than to resume their physical relationship—something that would lead to yet more heartbreak.

Would she have the willpower to resist him?

CHAPTER EIGHT

EXACTLY three days later Katy found herself standing on the balcony of a hotel in the Spanish city of Seville.

The heat of the summer sun, even so late in the afternoon, was almost unbearable and she retreated into the welcome cool of her suite.

Stepping away from the balcony, she stared in awe at the room again, wondering how she could possibly have been booked into anything so sumptuous.

This was the first time she'd attended a medical conference in her career, but she'd assumed that relatively junior doctors like herself usually had to make do with pretty humble accommodation.

But there was nothing humble about her room. It reflected the Moorish influence on the city, with a décor so opulent that it made her feel as though she should be dressed in seven veils and prepared for a harem.

As she reached for her suitcase, there was a knock on the door and one of the hotel staff delivered her a letter.

Surprised, she tore it open and immediately recognised the bold, black scrawl.

'Be ready at 7. Jago.'

Her fingers tightened on the note and her heart rate sped into the distance. It was typical of Jago to arrogantly assume she'd be willing to spend an evening with him. And equally typical for him not to disclose what he had in mind.

The conference didn't officially start until tomorrow, but she knew that there was a welcoming dinner for the delegates.

He must be planning to escort her to that.

Suddenly she had butterflies in her stomach. She shouldn't go with him. She really, really shouldn't...

But she'd been planning to attend the dinner anyway and it would certainly be more relaxing to be with someone she knew, she reasoned. And they'd be surrounded by other delegates. What could possibly happen?

Helplessly acknowledging just how much she wanted to spend an evening with Jago, she gave a sigh.

Why not?

Just one evening and she'd make sure that she slept in her own room at the end of the night.

Not wanting to dwell on her decision for too long, she glanced at her watch.

If he was collecting her at seven then she had less than two hours to find something suitable to wear and get ready for the evening, and she hadn't even had time to unpack yet.

She opened her case and gave a gasp of surprise.

Instead of the businesslike dresses and co-ordinates that she'd packed in blacks and other muted colours, the case contained what appeared to be an entire summer wardrobe in vibrant, eye-catching colours and designs.

At first she thought that there'd been a mix up with her luggage but then she saw the note attached to the inside of the case.

'Time to stop locking yourself away. Enjoy. Love, Libby and Alex.'

She sat down on the bed with a plop. Somehow Libby had managed to switch the entire contents of her case without her noticing. Instead of her usual safe, understated wardrobe, she was confronted by a rainbow of bright, sexy clothing.

She swallowed as she fingered the first item of clothing that came to hand. It was a strappy top in aquamarine, which came with a silk skirt in myriad complementary colours.

Rummaging further into the case, she found a selection of similar clothes. Short, flirty summer dresses, skirts, T-shirts, even a very brief bikini.

Spreading them out on the bed, Katy stared at them helplessly. They were the sort of clothes she would never have selected for herself. The woman who wore them would be confident of her feminine appeal and happy to flaunt it. *But she wasn't that sort of woman.*

Or was she?

Without intending to, she found herself picking up the strappy top and holding it against her as she looked at herself in the mirror. The colour seemed to intensify the blue of her eyes and the soft blush of her complexion.

She smiled, suddenly feeling like a little girl dressing up.

Why shouldn't she wear it? She wasn't speaking at the conference. In fact, she wasn't doing anything except listening to other people and learning. Apart from Jago, no one knew who she was. She didn't have to create an impression. She didn't need to worry about being taken seriously.

Telling herself that wanting to look good had absolutely nothing to do with the fact that she was spending the evening with Jago, she tugged the top over her head and frowned as she noticed the way it clung to the roundness of her breasts. For someone who usually wore loose shirts in nondescript colours it seemed incredibly daring.

Feeling ridiculously light-headed, she pulled on the skirt and rummaged for something to put on her feet, smiling as she found a pair of Libby's favourite designer shoes at the bottom of the case.

The heels were ridiculous and she'd probably break an ankle, but they matched the outfit perfectly.

Having brushed her hair until it poured down her back in a silken curtain, she risked a glance in the mirror.

She looked…different.

Bold. Feminine.

Sexy.

Not at all the way she'd have chosen to look for an evening out with a man as lethally attractive as Jago Rodriguez.

What was she doing?

Jago strode into the hotel lobby at five minutes to seven and made straight for the lifts.

When he'd written the note he'd been banking on the fact that Katy would be feeling vulnerable in a strange city. He was acutely aware that nothing else would have induced her to spend an evening with him so he was bracing himself for yet another rejection when he rapped on her door.

The door opened and he found himself frozen into immobility.

She looked stunning.

She was wearing something stretchy and blue that brought out the colour of her eyes and clung provocatively to the soft curve of her breasts. Her skirt was long enough to be decent but short enough to reveal a tempting expanse of her perfect legs. And as for her hair...

Feeling himself harden in an instinctive male reaction, Jago fought the temptation to power her back inside the bedroom and lay her down on the nearest suitable surface.

Conscious that he was staring, he made a supreme effort to pull himself together, wondering what had happened in the few hours since he'd last seen her.

As long as he'd known her, Katy had always tried to conceal her looks. *But not tonight.* Tonight for some reason she'd chosen to put her incredible beauty on display.

'*You're staring.*'

Her husky tones penetrated the haze of lustful male appreciation and he jerked his eyes to hers, noticing with no small degree of satisfaction that she was trembling.

'And who can blame me? You look stunning, *querida.*'

'Do you think so?' She glanced at him and then looked

down at her feet. 'To be honest, I'm not sure if I can even walk in these. They were Libby's choice. The minx switched the contents of my suitcase.'

'Did she now?' Jago's eyes narrowed as he contemplated the meaning behind those words.

So he wasn't the only one who was trying to unveil the real Katy.

Her cheeks were pink and she smiled apologetically. 'I don't usually wear heels. I dwarf whoever I'm with.'

'Then it's fortunate that I'm tall,' he said with amusement, extending an arm. 'For the record, I'm glad you've left your hair loose.'

She gave a wry smile. 'I thought it would save you the trouble of pulling it down.'

'Very wise.' His eyes gleamed. 'Shall we go?'

She locked the room and followed him into the lift. 'Are we going to the conference dinner?'

'No.' He could see the taut outline of her nipples under the clinging fabric of her top and he had to stop himself pushing her against the side of the lift and taking her in the most primitive way possible. His whole body ached with the strength of his arousal and he closed his eyes and tried to apply logic to the situation.

He was about to walk across a hotel lobby in full view of a large number of staff, not to mention guests, and if he didn't think about something other than Katy spread beneath him then he was going to be arrested.

'So where are we going?'

How could she be so totally unaware of the effect she had on him? Was she really still as innocent as she'd been at eighteen? Jago gritted his teeth and concentrated hard on the buttons of the lifts. Surely they were suitably boring?

'I'm taking you to see the real Seville.'

The lift doors opened and Jago ran a hand through his dark hair, feeling thoroughly out of control. His feelings intensified as he intercepted the appreciative male stares that Katy received as they walked out of the hotel. Growling under his breath, Jago took her hand possessively.

The down side of her looking so stunning was that everyone else thought she looked stunning, too. For the first time he had some understanding as to why she chose to conceal her beauty. Katy could stop traffic in the dark.

They walked for a short distance and then he pushed open the door of a well-known bar.

Katy looked at him in confusion. 'Are we eating here?'

Jago laughed. 'This is a tapas bar, *querida*. In Spain we eat dinner late in the evening. Tapas is a way of preventing us from dying of hunger. It's an integral part of Spanish culture.'

'Oh.' She looked interested and pleased and settled herself on a stool by the bar, looking round her with wide-eyed enthusiasm. 'I've had tapas in London but I don't suppose it's the same thing.'

'Similar, but each bar here will have its own speciality,' he told her, gesturing to some of the dishes that kept appearing.

'Translate, please.' She looked at him expectantly and he fought the impulse to kiss her.

That was going to have to wait until they were back in the privacy of their hotel.

With considerable difficulty he turned his attention to the food. 'Do you trust me to order?'

She nodded and he spoke in rapid Spanish, selecting a number of dishes that he thought she'd enjoy.

'This is a variety of olive grown in Seville,' he told her, lifting an olive towards her soft mouth. 'It's called Manzanilla.'

She tasted it and smiled. 'It's delicious.'

'And this is Chorizo—a spicy sausage.'

Katy nodded. 'I've seen it in the supermarket at home.'

'Not the same,' Jago assured her with an exaggerated shudder. 'This is fat and juicy, try it.'

She chewed slowly and he suppressed a groan as he watched her lips move. Food became unbearably erotic when Katy was involved.

'You look great in that outfit,' he said gruffly, helping himself to some food. 'Libby knows what will suit you.'

'She also knows that I never wear this sort of thing,' Katy confessed, glancing down at herself with a rueful expression. 'I feel…conspicuous. As if I'm shouting, "Look at Me," at the top of my voice.'

'Katy, you're the most beautiful woman I've ever seen,' he said dryly, 'and the same goes for every man in this room. You could be wearing a bin bag and people would stare.'

She looked shaken by his compliment and he resisted the urge to yank her off the bar stool and carry her back to the hotel.

For a minute she didn't reply and then she lifted her eyes to his and he saw the sadness there.

'But sometimes people don't see any further than the way I look.' Her voice was so soft he had to strain to hear her.

'It's true that the human race has an uncomfortable tendency to judge on appearances,' he agreed, forking another morsel into his mouth. 'But being beautiful must surely work to your advantage.'

She shook her head. 'Not always. Take being a doctor. To begin with, all anyone sees is my blonde hair and the fact that I'm so tall. That's why I wear flat shoes—'

'And glasses,' he finished, and she nodded.

'The glasses were Alex's idea. He has this thing that women look more academic if they wear glasses, and I think he's right. If I scrape my hair back, wear something sober and put on my glasses, people take me more seriously.'

Jago decided against confessing that he wanted to drag her into bed whatever she was wearing. He found her naïvety incredibly sweet.

'Is that why you gave up modelling?'

'Partly. It was so shallow. And incredibly boring.' She pulled a face. 'And I hated the falseness of it all—people just wanting to be seen with you because you were a model.'

Thinking about it, it didn't surprise him that she'd given it up. He'd been out with enough models in his time to know that she was much too gentle and sweet to survive long in such a cut-throat profession.

Suddenly he found himself fascinated by every tiny detail of her life and he realised that they were talking about things they'd never talked about before. Eleven years ago their relationship had been based on a searing mutual attraction that had pretty much eclipsed all other aspects of their relationship. Which was why he'd been so hasty to believe her father. If he'd known more about her thoughts and feelings, he would have known that such an action would have been totally out of character.

'So when did you decide on medical school?'

'When Alex started talking about it.' She took a sip of her drink. 'It sounded so exciting and my exam results were almost as good as his so I didn't see why I couldn't do it, too.'

'But your father objected.'

Her face lost its colour and he felt his shoulders tense. Was she really so afraid of her father?

'He had other plans for me.'

'And he didn't think that you should be allowed to decide your future for yourself?'

'That isn't the way my father works, as you should know by now. He's very controlling.'

Jago frowned. 'Is he the same with Alex?'

'He's the same with everyone, but he has absolutely no

influence over my brother.' She gave a wry smile. 'My father has met his match in Alex. They clash like herd bulls fighting over territory.'

'And Libby?'

Katy gave a rueful smile. 'We each handle him in a different way. Libby takes the confrontational approach and provokes him constantly so the atmosphere is pretty charged when they're together.'

'Whereas you go for the path of least conflict?'

She hesitated. 'Let's just say that over the years I've learned that it's better not to antagonise him. But that doesn't mean that I don't stand up for myself on the big issues.' She tilted her head to one side and her blonde hair shone under the lights. 'What about you? Why did you go into medicine?'

Jago made a huge effort and dragged his eyes away from her hair. It was confession time. Just how honest did he dare be with her? For the first time since they'd met again, she seemed to be relaxing with him and he certainly didn't want to destroy that. On the other hand, he was rapidly coming to the conclusion that having secrets definitely didn't work. Especially not with someone as honest as Katy. 'I'd been thinking about it for a while,' he hedged, and then he caught her puzzled glance and let out a long breath. 'You're not going to like what I tell you, *querida*.'

Her blue eyes widened, and he reflected grimly that telling the truth certainly wasn't the easy option.

'After he showed me the photographs, your father suggested that it would be better for everybody if I left the company and started afresh somewhere else,' he said curtly, aware that the facts looked uncomfortably incriminating. 'You have to understand I was very hurt by the photographs. Had I stayed with the company it was inevitable that we would have run into each other again. I was only too pleased when your father encouraged me to leave.'

There was a long silence as she made the connection.

'He paid you off, didn't he?' Her voice was little more than a whisper. 'He showed you the photographs and then he paid you to leave.'

She was obviously more attuned to her father's tricks than he'd been.

'At the time I thought of it as a generous severance package,' he admitted not quite levelly, all too aware of the interpretation she would put on the facts.

Pale and taut, she slid off the bar stool and looked at him blankly.

'I'd already decided to train as a doctor and he offered me a good package,' Jago said, feeling the tension spread through his shoulders. 'It's standard practice in many companies. At the time I didn't think it had anything to do with my relationship with you. It was a business issue.'

'Not to my father. He didn't dare risk having you anywhere near me because he knew you'd find out what he'd done.' It was almost as if she was talking to herself and he felt maximum discomfort for the part he'd played in the destruction of their relationship eleven years previously. 'He was determined to keep us apart.'

Jago found himself unable to argue with that. Even he was stunned by the level of manipulation to which her father had stooped and he thought of himself as a fairly cynical guy.

Katy stared at him in disbelief. 'You accepted money from him in return for an agreement not to see me again.'

He stiffened. 'That's not true. Your name was never mentioned in connection with the money. That was a business issue.'

'You're deluding yourself.' Her eyes glistened with hurt. 'He paid you off, Jago. And you took the money.'

'There seemed no reason not to.'

'You were already rich, Jago. I know that. How much money was enough?' she said shakily. 'How much did it cost him to get you to walk away from me?'

Jago swore softly in Spanish. 'It wasn't like that.'

'My life fell apart when you left but you were so self-absorbed, so wrapped up in your own emotions and feelings that you didn't stop to think about me even for a minute. You took the money and ran. Literally.'

Aware that the warmth of the atmosphere had plunged several degrees below zero, and extremely disconcerted by her less than flattering interpretation of the facts, Jago attempted to salvage the situation.

'We were having a pleasant evening before we started talking about your father,' he said calmly. 'Can we just forget it?'

'I don't think so.' Her breathing was rapid and she lifted her chin. 'You've just reminded me why I shouldn't have said yes to going out with you tonight. You are arrogant and selfish and we don't share the same beliefs and values. Goodnight, Jago.'

Reaching the frustrating conclusion that women were definitely from another planet, Jago made an abortive attempt to prevent her from leaving but she was too quick for him, heading for the door as fast as she could reasonably manage in Libby's ridiculously high-heeled shoes.

CHAPTER NINE

STILL sniffing back tears, Katy slid out of her skirt and dragged off the clingy blue top that she'd put on with such breathless anticipation. Feeling in need of a warm drink, she ordered from room service and then padded into the bathroom in her underwear to run herself a bath.

Of all the men on the planet, she'd chosen to fall in love with someone so totally wrapped up in himself that he didn't even know there was a world around him.

She emptied the entire contents of the miniature bubble bath bottle into the water and watched while it frothed.

Jago could be so charming when he wanted to be, but it was all part of his strategy for getting her back into his bed. And she'd nearly fallen for it.

Removing her underwear, she stepped into the water, reflecting that the sooner she learned to apply cynicism to her judgement of people, the happier she'd be. For a short time she'd been fooled by his trick of seeming so interested in her family and her feelings, and it had only been the shocking discovery that he'd actually accepted money from her father to remove himself from her life that had reminded her that this was the man who'd given absolutely no thought to her feelings whatsoever.

They said that everyone had their price, but it was agonising to realise that it was true.

In his own way, Jago shared many traits with her father. He was driven and ruthless and all he thought about was money.

It didn't matter how much she loved him. She'd be crazy to start a relationship with him again.

Hearing a knock on the door, she stepped out of the bath

and wrapped herself in a fluffy white bathrobe. She opened the door to receive the drink she'd ordered and found Jago lounging there, his expression hidden under lowered lashes.

'I've come to the conclusion that we should both stop talking, *querida*,' he drawled, planting a lean brown hand in the middle of the door to prevent her shutting it in his face. 'Words can so easily be misinterpreted, which is why we're moving on to actions.'

She backed away from him, acutely conscious of her still damp, naked body underneath the softness of her white, fluffy bathrobe.

'I was having a bath.'

'I can tell. The ends of your hair are wet,' he murmured, his dark gaze roaming with appreciation over the golden strands.

Without her even being aware of how it happened, he was inside her room with the door firmly locked behind him.

Paralysed by the hot, quivering excitement that erupted inside her, she reminded herself repeatedly that he was a selfish, egotistical, thoroughly objectionable male who would break her heart again if she were to be so stupid as to let him.

'There is just no way you're marrying Freddie,' he imparted thickly, hauling her against him with all the finesse of a wild animal. In fact, she realised with some considerable degree of shock, Jago didn't seem controlled at all. The hand that brushed her damp hair away from her brow was decidedly unsteady, and his breathing was far from even.

His mouth fused with hers, his kiss rough and demanding, and despite all her resolutions Katy just melted.

She kissed him back, her fingers resting on the hard muscle of his chest and then sliding upwards round his strong neck. Wild excitement exploded inside her. He felt *so* good.

He cupped her face, his tongue teasing hers, exploring

every part of her sensitive mouth, and suddenly she found she was shivering.

He lifted his head with a reluctant groan, and hugged her close. 'Are you cold?'

'I'm not cold.' She looked at him with helpless longing, knowing that she ought to tell him to leave, but totally unable to do it.

His mouth descended to hers again and this time she felt his hands on her shoulders, divesting her of her fluffy bath-robe with electrifying efficiency.

'Jago!' Suddenly aware that she was naked and he was still fully clothed, she pulled away from him, but he swept her into his arms and deposited her on the bed before she could even consider covering herself.

'You have the most incredible body,' he muttered, fumbling with the buttons of his shirt with considerably less finesse than he'd shown when he'd undressed *her*.

His shirt hit the floor and she stared, feasting on the sight of his muscular chest and flat abdomen.

'You could help me,' Jago suggested huskily, but Katy found she couldn't move.

She just lay there, watching him, flattened to the bed by an excitement and anticipation so intense that it was almost painful.

She wanted him. *Badly.*

Every single part of her body ached for him to possess her.

Gloriously naked, Jago moved over her with the lithe movement of a jungle cat and all the confidence of a male with the upper hand.

'Are you going to speak, *querida*?' His soft, teasing tone made her insides melt and she shook her head, her eyes dropping to his incredible sexy mouth.

She was beyond speech.

With a soft laugh he lowered his head to within an inch

of her mouth, hovering tantalisingly close, allowing their breath to mingle but still not touching her.

A slow burn began inside her and she shifted her hips, desperate to relieve the tension.

His attention drawn by her wanton movements, he gave an earthy groan and crushed her mouth under his.

His kiss was hot and hard and intensely sexual and she clutched at him desperately, writhing against him in an attempt to get closer still.

Breathing hard, he detached himself and worked his way down her body, using his incredibly skilled fingers to torment the hardened peaks of her full breasts.

She arched and cried out in desperation and his mouth replaced his clever fingers, his tongue teasing the damp tips with an erotic expertise that made her squirm.

She could feel his breath warming her and then he sucked her into the darkness of his mouth and she gasped in disbelief as she felt the sensation deep in her pelvis.

Instinctively she parted her thighs and immediately his fingers were there, exploring and teasing her in the most intimate way possible. He knew exactly how to touch her to create maximum sensation and soon she was beyond modesty or control.

She felt totally wanton, agitated and feverish, and he continued to torture her with pleasure, teasing her until she gasped his name in an agony of longing, desperate for him to give her the fulfillment she craved.

Driven totally wild by his leisurely exploration of her body, she twisted under him in a frenzy of almost unbearable anticipation, but he shifted his weight and held her still, refusing to give her the satisfaction she sought.

'Jago, *please*...' Her whole body was burning with erotic sensation and she was sobbing now, begging for him to stop tormenting them both. The excitement was intolerable, a fiery ache deep inside her that threatened to consume her whole being with its intensity.

He stared down into her flushed face, his eyes dark with a depth of arousal that made her catch her breath.

'Jago…'

'*Tell me you want me,*' he said thickly, stroking her silken hair away from her damp skin. 'I need to hear you say it, *querida.*'

Trapped by the raw emotion she saw in his eyes, she could barely speak.

'I want you—*now.*'

He muttered something in Spanish and slid a strong arm under her hips, moving her under him. Her breath came in pants as she felt the silken thrust of his arousal against the very heart of her and then he drove into her with a hard thrust that brought a gasp of ecstasy to her lips.

She cried out his name and he plunged deeper still and suddenly all she could feel was heat.

The scorch of his mouth as it covered hers.

The burn of his body as he moved with a pagan rhythm that drove her to a level of excitement that she'd never experienced before.

And the fire within her.

Desperate to be closer still, she arched against him and he gave an earthy groan and withdrew before sliding into her again with a force that made her sob with ecstasy.

She was no longer in control of anything. She wasn't aware of anything except the explosive excitement that consumed her body as he thrust hard into her with a rhythmic force that drove her to a state of such intense arousal that it seemed too much to bear. Arching against him, she slid her hands over the smooth muscle of his back, urging him closer still, her body screaming for completion. And then suddenly, when she thought she could bear it no longer, he sent her flying into a shattering climax which seemed to last for ever, her whole body unravelling in an ecstasy intensified by the shuddering throb of his own release.

Completely wiped out by the experience, Katy lay still,

aware of the pounding of his heart against hers, of the damp warmth of their bodies as they clung together so intimately.

His breathing still uneven, he shifted his weight and rolled onto his back, taking her with him, and suddenly she was hideously aware of just how out of control she'd been.

She squeezed her eyes tightly shut in a rush of embarrassment.

What had happened to her?

For goodness' sake, she'd virtually begged the man!

Mortified by the intensity of her response to him, she rolled away from him, only to find herself dragged back against his hard, muscular body.

'*Stop* trying to create distance between us,' he murmured huskily, sliding his fingers through the length of her hair with all the smug satisfaction of a man who'd just got exactly what he'd wanted.

Desperation spread through her body like a flood. Would she always be this vulnerable to him?

'Sex doesn't change anything between us.'

'Shut up,' he groaned, rolling her under him and proceeding to kiss her again. 'You *definitely* talk too much.'

So instead of talking, she found herself kissing him back and this time he took her with agonising slowness, each slow, deliberate thrust designed to drive her to the very heights of desperation. Unable to believe that he could arouse her again so quickly, Katy closed her eyes and gave herself up to sensation, totally unable to control her response.

'You feel so good,' Jago groaned, and her eyes flew wide and clashed with his as he thrust into her with surprising gentleness.

Transfixed by the look of male appreciation that she caught in his eyes, her stomach tumbled over itself and she felt swamped with love. He was just so amazing in bed. It would have been so very easy to believe that he loved her.

She felt her body tingle as he aroused her yet again to a

state of mindless abandonment, but yet again he chose to delay satisfaction until their bodies were both screaming with unfulfilled excitement before driving them both, gasping, to a ferocious climax.

The first shafts of morning sunlight were fingering their way through the open window when she finally fell asleep, and when she awoke he was gone.

After a day of back-to-back presentations and discussions, during which she'd watched with helpless hunger as Jago had wowed the extremely high-powered audience with his cool intellect, Katy returned to the hotel and opened the door of her room.

She was immediately assaulted by the powerful scent of flowers. And not just one bunch of flowers. Her room seemed to contain the entire year's stock of an average florist.

Taken aback, she walked into the room, her eyes focusing on a card which had been left on the table.

She picked it up and read it.

'You look very beautiful when you're asleep. J.'

They were from Jago.

Jago, who'd never sent her flowers before.

Still reeling over the sheer volume of blooms, she heard the door of her room close suddenly and turned to find him standing there.

Her heart stumbled in her chest and she felt her whole body react to his powerful presence.

He was staggeringly good-looking.

To even *think* that she could resist him was to totally underestimate the impact of his explosive brand of sexuality.

He removed his jacket with a shrug of his broad shoulders and jerked off his tie. 'It's been a very long and very boring day, *querida*,' he murmured huskily, dropping the tie on the bed with careless disregard for its future appearance. 'Concentrating on my slides was a formidable challenge. All I could think of was getting back to the hotel and being with you.'

Katy stared at him helplessly.

All he could think about was sex. He was just *so* basic and she really ought to be protesting, but already he'd undone the buttons on his shirt and her mouth dried as the fabric fell apart to reveal a tantalising glimpse of his tanned, muscular chest. Unable to help herself, her eyes traced the dark hairs as they travelled down and into the waistband of his trousers.

'If you want to help, please, feel free,' he teased her gently, and she felt the colour touch her cheeks.

'Jago, we ought to talk.'

They hadn't resolved anything and she just *knew* he was going to hurt her again. After all, never, despite all his commands that she give up Freddie, had he once implied that he felt anything for her other than lust.

She had to tell him that, despite what had happened between them the night before, nothing had changed.

She still had no intention of renewing her relationship with him in the long term.

'Talking never seems to clear the air between us,' he pointed out thickly, moving towards her with effortless elegance and tipping her backwards onto the bed.

He came down on top of her, confident and fully in control, and she realised helplessly that he was fighting the battle with the strongest weapon in his armoury. His ability to excite her to a state of mindless desperation.

And he was winning. Despite all her reservations about the future, the truth was that this was *now*, and she wanted him *so* much.

Suddenly losing her natural shyness, she stroked her fingers through the curling hair on his chest, loving the feel of his hard muscles. He was just so strong. Her breathing jerky, she followed the line of silky dark hair with the tips of her fingers, pausing as it vanished into the waistband of his trousers. She felt him suck in a breath and realised that for once he seemed uncertain.

With a smile that was pure female seduction, she dealt with the rest of his clothing, and if it wasn't done with quite the finesse he'd managed, neither of them seemed to notice.

Certainly not Jago, whose shocked exclamation had turned to a groan of earthy satisfaction as she explored him with incredible intimacy. Aware of the reaction of his body, she drove him wild with her mouth and tongue until he dragged her away from him with a rough groan.

He looked at her with a glazed expression and she derived considerable satisfaction from the look of stunned amazement on his handsome face. He looked positively shell-shocked. Feeling immensely satisfied that she'd finally managed to make him lose control, she leaned forward to kiss him and he caught her in lean, strong hands and moved her so that she was straddling him.

Still breathing heavily, he slid her flimsy dress up to her hips and moved the dampened silk of her panties to one side with lean fingers.

Shocked by the revelation that he didn't even intend to undress her, Katy trembled with anticipation, a gasp of helpless excitement wrenched from her as she felt him position her to receive him.

She felt the silken throb of his erection against her and then her eyes flew wide as he slid into her, hard and strong, holding her writhing hips still as he ground deep inside her.

Cheeks flushed, lips parted, Katy moaned as she felt him move, unbelievably aroused by the force of his possession.

It was over quickly, both of them reaching a climax of such unbelievable intensity that they clung together for endless moments before Jago smoothed her tangled blonde hair away from her face and snuggled her in his arms.

She closed her eyes in disbelief, hardly knowing herself.

'You've never done that before,' he said softly, shifting slightly so that she was forced to look at him. 'You were always much too shy.'

She knew it was true and felt hot colour touch her cheeks. Somehow making love with Jago felt different now that she was older.

At eighteen she'd been hideously self-conscious and gauche and she was only now beginning to realise how careful he'd been with her, how much he must have been holding back. Their love-making had possessed none of the wildness that he'd displayed in the last twenty-four hours.

He touched her cheek with gentle fingers, his expression thoughtful. 'We will be checking out tomorrow,' he told her. 'We're visiting my family.'

She stilled in his arms. His family?

Jago always avoided questions about his family and she knew better than to ask.

Why was he taking her to meet them?

And why was she excited at the prospect?

This wasn't what she wanted, was it? Whatever she felt for him, she didn't *want* to renew her relationship with Jago.

She closed her eyes tightly, knowing that she should send him back to his room and go straight home to England without meeting his family.

But how could she when she was loving every minute of their time together?

Why shouldn't she just enjoy herself for now? Why shouldn't she just make the most of this time in Spain, she reasoned, ignoring the tiny voice in her head that warned her this wasn't real.

She'd have plenty of time to face reality when they returned to England.

They left the following afternoon, immediately after the last lecture.

Having cleared her room and packed, Katy made her way

to the foyer of the hotel, intending to check out before
going with Jago.

The hotel manager met her at the marble reception desk.
'Everything has been taken care of,' he said in heavily ac-
cented English.

Katy stared at him in confusion. What did he mean—
taken care of? How could her bill have been taken care of?

The hotel manager suddenly looked over her shoulder
and smiled warmly. Following his gaze, Katy turned to find
Jago approaching. Just looking at him made her legs turn
to jelly. He was so good-looking it was almost indecent.
Surely no one man should be blessed with such incredibly
good looks, she thought helplessly. Didn't he have a single
flaw? He was wearing jeans and a black polo shirt that
emphasised his dark, exotic brand of masculinity.

Reaching her side, he gave her a brief smile and then
turned his attention to the hotel manager, conversing in
rapid Spanish which she found totally incomprehensible.

The two men obviously enjoyed a good relationship and
suddenly they were descended on by staff who carried her
luggage towards the door of the hotel, leaving them to follow.

'You shouldn't have had to carry your case downstairs,'
Jago muttered as he strode towards the entrance of the hotel, leaving her struggling to keep up with him.

She looked at him with some amusement. 'Jago, I can
carry my own case!'

'Not in this hotel,' he growled, pushing open the swing
doors and snapping his fingers.

Katy's mouth fell open as a stunning black Ferrari pulled
up at the entrance.

Accepting the keys with a nod of thanks, Jago shot her
a satisfied smile. 'Your carriage, *senorita*.'

In awe of the sleek lines of the beautiful car, she slid
inside, feeling herself enveloped by the sumptuous leather
interior.

'Wow…'

He slid into the driver's seat next to her and smiled at her childish exclamation.

'I agree,' he said, laughter in his voice. 'This car is definitely "wow".'

She couldn't resist teasing him. 'Boys with toys, Jago?'

'Of course.'

'Everyone's staring,' she muttered, clearly conscious of the looks they were receiving.

'That's why I bought the car,' he drawled. 'It increases my street cred no end.'

He pulled out into the traffic and she looked at him curiously. 'It's yours?'

'It is mine. I keep it here for my trips home.'

He kept a Ferrari just for his trips home. She couldn't contain her questions any longer. 'Do you often come home?'

'As often as I can.'

She rolled her eyes at his answer, which was typical Jago. 'Do you ever give anything away?'

His smile was totally unapologetic. 'As little as possible.' There was a silence as he negotiated a particularly busy junction and then he spoke again. 'I come back to Spain about once every two months—sometimes more if I have to.'

'To stay with your family?'

He hesitated. 'I have business interests in Seville.'

'But you're a doctor.'

He smiled. 'How can you be the child of Charles Westerling and be so totally lacking in commercial awareness?'

She blushed and looked away. She hated business and found her father's approach to business ruthless and distasteful.

'Working with your father taught me just how fragile

financial success can be,' Jago said quietly. 'After I left his company I used the money I'd made to invest in various business ventures in Spain. I own the hotel where we just stayed.'

He owned it?

Katy's head spun round and she stared at him. 'Is that why I had such a fabulous room?'

'You liked it?' He gave her a smile that was thoroughly male. 'Good. I thought you would enjoy it.'

'And somebody had settled my bill.'

'There was no bill, *querida*,' he said smoothly. 'You were my guest.'

She digested this information. 'Where did the other delegates stay?'

He gave a careless shrug. 'At various hotels around the city.'

So he'd made sure that they were staying separately from the others.

She took a deep breath. 'The money you invested—'

'Was not the money your father gave me as a severance package,' he drawled, his voice low and deep. 'I can read you like a book. I used that for something entirely separate, as I hope to show you in a few hours.'

Not wanting to threaten the delicate truce between them, Katy relaxed back in her seat and enjoyed the Spanish countryside.

They drove along dusty roads, passing olive groves and almond trees, and Katy suddenly felt happier than she had for ages.

Whatever he'd done in the past, she couldn't help loving him and just being with him made her feel good.

They'd been driving for about an hour when they approached a small village and Katy noticed a crowd gathered by the side of the road.

'Stop, Jago!' she cried out, and put a hand on his arm.

'Something's wrong. Someone's on the ground—there must have been an accident.'

Jago responded immediately, pulling into the side of the road. In an instant Katy was out of the car.

A young woman was lying on the pavement, clutching her throat, struggling for air.

Her heart thumping frantically against her chest, Katy dropped to her knees, making a diagnosis without even the briefest hesitation. She knew instantly what she was seeing. *She'd seen it before.*

'Get away from her and give her some air,' she said, aware that they were looking at her blankly. Fortunately, at that moment Jago appeared by her side and spoke in fluent Spanish. The crowd parted instantly.

'She's in anaphylactic shock,' Katy muttered. 'Her lips and tongue are swollen and she's wheezing badly. Ask them what happened. Has she been stung?'

There was a rapid exchange of Spanish and then Jago hunkered down beside her. 'They say that she was stung by a bee a few minutes ago.' He sucked in a breath as he looked at the young woman. 'She's bad and I don't have anything in my car.'

'My handbag.' Katy looked up at him, her blonde hair flopping over her face. She scraped it away with an impatient hand. 'Get my handbag, quickly.'

Without arguing, Jago did as she requested, returning in seconds with the bag she'd left in the footwell of the car.

She snapped it open and rummaged to find what she needed.

'Where was she stung?'

She addressed her question to Jago, who translated quickly and then turned back to Katy.

'Above her eye.'

'We've got to get that sting out.' Katy located the sting and then removed it quickly with some forceps that she always kept in her bag.

'We need to give her some adrenaline.' She reached into her bag again and removed a small box that she always carried. 'I presume someone has called an ambulance?'

'It's on its way,' Jago said, looking at her in stunned disbelief. 'What have you got there?'

'Adrenaline and hydrocortisone,' Katy muttered. 'I always carry it.'

Aware of the horrified murmurings of the crowd, she jabbed the woman in the arm and delivered the adrenaline as fast as she could. Then she picked up the other syringe, brisk and competent.

She knew exactly what needed to be done and she knew that it needed to be done quickly.

'Can you squeeze her arm for me?'

Jago obliged and Katy searched for a vein and then injected the hydrocortisone.

Dropping the empty syringe back into the box, she then moved the woman into the recovery position with Jago's help.

'Her breathing's improving, but just to be on the safe side I'm going to give her some chlorpheniramine as well.' She rummaged in her bag again, aware that Jago was watching her with amazement.

'She's starting to recover.' He checked the woman's pulse. 'This is unbelievable. Do you carry an entire drug cabinet in your handbag?'

Despite the seriousness of the situation, she managed a smile. 'I happen to be an expert in this particular emergency. There's nothing else we can do now. She needs high-dose oxygen. I wish that ambulance would hurry up.'

Even as the words left her mouth they saw the ambulance approaching.

'She needs to be admitted,' Katy said, dropping the remains of the injections back into the box and returning it to her handbag. 'Twenty per cent of patients relapse within eight to twelve hours. Better make sure they know that.'

The moment the words left her mouth she coloured. Why was she telling him that? Jago would almost certainly be aware of the fact.

Jago was speaking to the ambulance crew in Spanish and suddenly an oxygen cylinder appeared.

By now the young woman was sitting up, looking decidedly shaky and pale but very much alive.

An older woman burst into tears and flung her arms around a startled Katy.

'She's the woman's mother,' Jago said softly, a strange expression in his dark eyes. 'She says that you saved her daughter's life and she will always be in your debt.'

He spoke to the woman and she nodded and gave Katy a final hug before releasing her.

Suddenly the whole crowd was swarming round her and Katy looked at Jago in mute appeal.

He grinned and shouldered his way through to her. 'You're a bit of a heroine.'

'I just did what anyone would have done,' she mumbled, and he lifted an eyebrow.

'Most people don't carry an entire drug cabinet around with them.'

She smiled self-consciously and watched as they loaded the woman into the ambulance. 'Can we go now?'

'If that's what you want.'

He took her hand and led her through the crowd and she slid into the Ferrari with relief, feeling her limbs start to shake.

'Are you all right?' He settled himself in the driver's seat and frowned at her. 'You look very pale all of a sudden.'

She took a deep breath and gave him a wobbly smile. 'I think it just hit me that it could have had a different ending. She had a very severe reaction.'

'She would have died if it hadn't been for you,' Jago said roughly, rubbing a hand over his face and letting out a long breath. 'All right. Enlighten me. Why the hell do you carry all those drugs in your handbag?'

'Because of Libby.'

His eyes narrowed. 'Libby?'

'My sister is severely allergic to bee stings,' Katy told him. 'She carries adrenaline herself but I've got so used to worrying about her whenever we're out together in summer that I've just got used to carrying a stock of drugs. Alex does the same.'

Jago shook his head. 'Unbelievable.' He surveyed her with amusement and no small degree of admiration. 'I thought you were no good at immediate care?'

A warm feeling spread inside her and she flushed, pleased by his praise. 'I just happened to know about anaphylactic shock because of Libby.'

'Well, you undoubtedly saved that girl's life,' he said softly. 'I certainly don't carry adrenaline in my boot, although from now on I think I might do just that.'

Two hours from Seville, Jago turned down a dusty track and Katy saw a beautiful traditional Spanish farmhouse.

'Oh—it's beautiful.' The dusty bricks were a warm shade of apricot and the dwelling was surrounded by a terrace shaded by vines.

The front door opened and she recognised Jago's mother Maria, the woman who had been her parents' housekeeper for several years.

She stood back while they greeted each other, wondering what Maria would make of her presence.

Would she be surprised to see her?

Releasing Jago and wiping her eyes, Maria caught sight of her and her face brightened. She said something to Jago in Spanish and then stepped forward and embraced Katy affectionately.

'As beautiful as ever.' She reached up a hand and touched Katy's cheek. 'You are so very fair.' She frowned at her son. 'You must be careful not to let her burn in this hot sun.'

Touched by the warmth of her welcome, Katy followed them inside the spacious farmhouse, through a traditional kitchen and out onto a large terrace shaded by vines. Sunlight dappled the long wooden table, which was laid for dinner.

A couple were seated at the table and Jago greeted them and introduced them to Katy.

'Juan and Rosita Ruiz.' He took Katy's hand and pulled her forward. 'My aunt and uncle. I'm afraid they speak very little English.'

'Hola.' Katy returned their greeting shyly, using her very limited Spanish, and soon she was seated at the table, enjoying the warmth of their hospitality.

They ate plump olives and lamb roasted in herbs, and drank the warmest, most delicious red wine she'd ever tasted, and soon she found herself relaxing.

Totally at home in her new surroundings, Katy found herself sneaking looks at Jago, marvelling at the change in him.

He lounged in his chair, long legs stretched out in front of him, more relaxed than she'd ever seen him, switching smoothly between Spanish and English so that he could communicate with everyone.

By the time they'd finished dinner it was late and Katy fell into bed exhausted.

She awoke the next morning and found Jago already in the kitchen, drinking coffee.

'Good morning.' He rose to his feet and gestured to the food on the table. 'Toasted bread, home-made jam and *café con leche*—milky coffee. Help yourself.'

She settled herself at the table, trying not to look at the dark shadow of his hard jaw. Her constant awareness of him was so intense that it was making her jumpy.

'I missed you last night.' He put a hand over hers and suddenly she had butterflies in her stomach.

'Jago—'

'My family are very traditional and I would in no way offend them by broadcasting our relationship,' he said quietly, pouring her coffee and handing it to her. 'On the other hand, if you are going to carry on looking at me with that totally dizzy expression on your face, we're going to have to go and find ourselves a barn, *querida*.'

She blushed hotly at his teasing reminder of their relationship eleven years earlier. After that first encounter they'd continued to meet in the barn and the surrounding fields, often spending the entire night entwined together.

She had too many knots in her stomach to eat and he shot her an amused look and stood up.

'If you've finished, go and put a hat on. We're going for a walk and my mother is worried that you'll damage that delicate English skin of yours.'

Wondering where he was taking her, Katy found the pretty hat that Libby had tucked into her case and joined him on the terrace.

There was no sign of Maria or Jago's aunt and they left the farmhouse and walked along a dusty track that eventually led to a river. In the early morning sunlight it glistened and danced over boulders and Katy smiled with delight.

'It's beautiful.' It was the clearest water she'd ever seen and she watched it with fascination. 'What a lovely place.'

'The river marks the boundary of our property,' Jago told her, stooping to pick up a stone and tossing it in the water.

She glanced around her, screwing up her eyes against the sun. It was still quite early and yet already she could feel the heat on her skin.

'I love it here.'

'Do you?' He turned her to face him, his eyes suddenly intent. 'I bought it with the money your father gave me when I left the company.' Suddenly his eyes were hard and his fingers tightened on her arm in an almost painful grip. 'When he suggested that I leave, he also made Maria homeless and jobless.'

Shocked by that sudden revelation, Katy felt her mouth dry. At the time she'd been so distraught about her own situation she hadn't thought to question what had happened to her parents' housekeeper. She'd known that her leaving had coincided with Jago's but she'd just assumed that it had been coincidence. How could she have been so naïve?

Suddenly she felt horribly sick. 'My father fired her?'

Jago's eyes were as hard as flint and his mouth tightened. 'Let's just say he made it impossible for her to stay.' He released her and turned to stare at the river. 'Your father was in possession of some information which he knew would hurt my mother.'

Katy's knees were trembling. 'What information?' It was a favourite trick of her father's. He somehow managed to find something on everyone.

Jago didn't respond immediately and the silence seemed to stretch into infinity.

Katy felt her heart plummet uncomfortably. Part of her didn't even want to know what her father had done, but she knew that there had been too many secrets between them already.

'Jago?'

'Maria isn't my mother.' He made the statement in a matter-of-fact voice. 'My real mother had me at nineteen, was married immediately and then proceeded to have affairs with anyone that crossed her path.'

Katy stared at him, mute. Maria wasn't his real mother? His mother had had affairs?

'The people of Andalucia are very traditional. In some ways quite backward,' he said dryly. 'Machismo still rules in this part of Spain.'

Katy found herself holding her breath, knowing that there was more to come.

'My father eventually heard of one of her affairs and he shot her.'

Katy gasped and lifted a hand to her mouth. 'Jago—no!'

'No one thought he meant to do it,' Jago said, his voice strangely flat. 'He was just so crazed with grief that he wasn't rational. When he realised that he'd killed her he turned the gun on himself.'

Shocked into silence, Katy sank down onto a rock and stared at him.

'It created a huge scandal, of course,' Jago said in a lifeless voice. 'I was six years old so I wasn't aware of much, but I realised that suddenly no one seemed to want to play with me.'

She licked her lips. 'So what happened?'

'Fortunately for me, my mother had two sisters who realised that I needed to be taken away if I was ever going to be able to lead a normal life. People in Andalucia have very long memories. Maria moved to England with me and took a job as a housekeeper. It was very brave of her. At the time she spoke hardly any English, but she thought her secret was safe in England.'

'But my father knew about it?'

'Of course.' Jago's mouth tightened and a muscle worked in his lean jaw. 'As you've pointed out before, your father knows everything. He kept the information to himself in case he ever needed it. And, of course, once I showed interest in his daughter, he knew that that time had come. There was no way he wanted that sort of scandal attached to his family.'

'Oh, my God.' Katy stared at him, understanding more clearly why her father had been so determined to keep them apart. A high-profile figure, her father only ever wanted to read good things about himself in the press. At the time she'd thought that his objection had stemmed from the fact that Jago wasn't English and didn't have the right pedigree, but obviously there had been so much more to it than that.

Jago was still talking. 'Once he successfully removed me from your life, he knew that he had to get rid of Maria too or he'd risk me running into you when I visited her.'

Katy shook her head and swallowed hard. 'I never knew. I never knew that Dad made her leave. When I came out of hospital she was gone and I was just told that she'd decided to go back to Spain. I'm so sorry.'

He shrugged dismissively. 'Not your fault and, to be honest, Maria was ready to leave. She wanted to go back home but didn't really have the means.' He gave a short laugh. 'Fortunately, those years working for your father in the bank gave me the means. I bought her this place and she lives here with her other sister and brother-in-law.'

'And the locals?'

'They were apparently impressed with the way she sacrificed her homeland to care for a small, vulnerable child. She's been accepted back into society and lives very happily here.'

Katy was digesting the full implication of his words. 'No wonder you were so upset when you thought I was having an affair.'

He gave a wry smile. 'As I said, *querida*, for me faithfulness is the minimum requirement in a relationship.'

And she could understand why.

He'd grown up with the knowledge that his whole family had been destroyed by the actions of his mother.

For the first time she saw those photographs as he must have seen them.

As the ultimate betrayal.

For a man with such a shocking secret buried in his past, was it really surprising that he'd overreacted?

'I'm sorry,' she whispered. 'I understand now why you reacted so strongly when you saw those photographs.'

He gave a twisted smile. 'As you pointed out, your father was a master at manipulation. He knew exactly how to extract the maximum response from me.'

Numb with despair, Katy looked around her, aware of the calm beauty of her surroundings and yet barely seeing it. 'I'm really so very sorry about everything. And I'm sorry about what my father did to your mother.'

She felt mortified. Embarrassed and horrified at this latest example of her father's utter ruthlessness.

'Your father was very thorough,' Jago observed, the expression in his dark eyes veiled by thick lashes. 'He didn't want me involved with you and he was prepared to go to any lengths to prevent it.'

'He succeeded,' Katy said sadly, reflecting on the utter devastation that his actions had caused.

'Maybe not. We seem to have found each other again.' Jago stepped towards her and cupped her face in his hands. 'You know that you can't marry Freddie. He is wrong for you, and if you'd loved him you never would have slept with me.'

Katy almost smiled at the irony of that self-satisfied statement. Only a week ago he had believed her capable of exactly that. But now she understood his sensitivity in that area.

'I'm not going to marry Freddie,' she said quietly. 'I ended it that night you came to the flat.'

There was a long silence and when he finally spoke his voice was hoarse. 'You *did* end it? But you didn't tell me—you let me think…' He broke off and dragged a hand through his dark hair. *'Why?'*

She swallowed. 'Because I wanted to keep you at a distance.'

He gave a groan and hauled her against him. 'Have you any idea what I went through, thinking that you were still going to marry him? It was torture. And it's never going to happen again.' He let go of her suddenly and cupped her face in his lean hands, his eyes fierce. 'I want you to marry *me*.'

Katy stilled, convinced that she must have misheard him. 'Pardon?'

'Perhaps I'll rephrase that.' His voice was low and velvety. 'You are going to marry me.'

Her heart stampeded against her chest wall. 'But why? Why would you want to marry me?'

There was only the briefest hesitation on his part. 'Because you and I are good together.'

Katy swallowed back her disappointment. He'd made no mention of love. Clearly what he'd meant had been that they were good together in bed.

'Good sex doesn't guarantee a good relationship, Jago.'

He frowned. 'I'm not just talking about the sex. There has always been something between us.' He looked at her warily, clearly out of his depth and struggling to express himself, and she loved him all the more for it.

He was so utterly hopeless at talking about his feelings. And perhaps that was understandable. After such an awful childhood it was hardly surprising that he'd come to rely very much on his own resources.

And he might not love her but *she* loved him.

Couldn't that be enough?

After all, she'd been prepared to marry Freddie without love on either side. Why shouldn't she marry Jago when she loved him so desperately?

She knew that she could never be happy with any other man.

She looked at him shyly. 'You're serious? You really want to marry me?'

In answer Jago lowered his head and kissed her thoroughly.

'I'm going to marry you,' he muttered against her lips.

'As soon as we get back to England. And this time we're going to just do it and not tell your father.'

She opened her mouth to point out that her father was bound to find out at some point, but he hauled her into his arms and all rational thought vanished into the Spanish sun.

CHAPTER TEN

THEY flew home the following day and Katy returned to work that afternoon feeling as though she was walking on air.

She was marrying Jago.

She still couldn't quite believe it.

They'd agreed to keep it quiet until Jago could make the arrangements and she'd readily agreed. After all, she hadn't advertised the fact that her relationship with Freddie had ended and she was more than a little uncomfortable about announcing that she was marrying another man so quickly.

She was checking a set of X-rays when Jago strolled up, dressed in a light grey suit that emphasised the width of his shoulders and the golden sheen of his skin. He looked incredibly handsome and thoroughly fed up.

'I have a meeting with the hospital management about staffing levels,' he murmured grittily, glancing at his watch with obvious irritation. 'I have only one thing to say to them and that is that I need more staff, but doubtless they'll make me sit there for hours, listening to arguments for reducing manpower to skeletal proportions.'

She smiled and then remembered that she had something to tell him. 'I just rang the paediatric ward to check on Molly. Libby says she's doing really well.'

A smile touched his firm mouth. 'That's good news. I'll try and see her on my way to this meeting.'

Katy gazed at him longingly and he gave a low growl and stepped closer.

'Stop looking at me like that or I'll forget where we are and commit an indecent act in a public place.'

164

She chuckled and pushed him away, glancing round quickly to check that no one had seen them.

'I'll be back as quickly as I can,' he muttered huskily, his mind very clearly not on his work. 'If there's a crisis, call me.'

With a last lingering look at her mouth he strode off down the corridor like a man on a mission, as lithe and agile as a panther and totally back in control.

Katy forced her mind back to work, finished checking the X-rays and then returned to the patient.

'These X-rays are fine, Mrs Maxwell,' she said, reflecting on how much her confidence had grown since she'd started working with Jago. Because he had such high standards, knowing that he believed her to be a good doctor meant so much more.

She saw a series of minor injuries and then, about an hour into her shift, Ambulance Control called to say that they were bringing in a patient with chemical burns.

Three of the other senior doctors were already dealing with a man who'd come off his motorbike and Katy was forced to call Jago's mobile. She was reluctant to disturb him but knew that she was going to need his help. The other doctors were already pushed to cope with the volume of emergencies that had bombarded the department all morning.

'He works in a glass factory but I have no idea what the chemical is,' she told him, trying to sound calm. 'I'm guessing it could be hydrofluoric acid.'

'You're probably right.' Jago's reply broke up slightly as the signal on his mobile faltered. 'Get him into Resus and irrigate it with lots of lukewarm water. I'll be right down. And, for goodness' sake wear gloves before you touch him.'

She heard the ambulance siren as she replaced the phone and dragged on a pair of gloves before hurrying to meet the paramedics as they pushed open the doors and wheeled in the stretcher.

The man was writhing on the trolley, groaning in agony from the severity of the burns inflicted by the chemical.

'He had an accident with hydrofluoric acid. It's over both legs. We irrigated it with copious volumes of water while we were at the factory,' the paramedic informed them, 'but we wanted to transfer him as fast as possible.'

As they moved him into Resus Jago appeared at Katy's side.

'Keep irrigating it,' he ordered immediately, seeing just how badly the man was burned. 'Get both legs under a tap and then rub in some 2.5 per cent calcium gluconate gel.'

He reached for a pair of gloves and tugged them on with grim-faced efficiency.

'Did someone call for calcium gluconate gel?' Like a miracle of efficiency and teamwork, Charlotte appeared beside them and they washed the burn repeatedly and then finally applied the gel to the burns.

'What exactly does this gel do?' Charlotte asked as they worked.

Katy glanced at her. 'In this case calcium gluconate acts as a neutraliser but you have to be careful with some chemical burns. If you attempt to neutralise the chemical you can create heat and make the burn worse. Hydrofluoric acid is the exception.'

'Really?' Charlotte looked at her in admiration and Jago smiled.

'Chemistry was obviously your thing, Dr Westerling.'

'I was always quite good at chemistry,' Katy said modestly, concentrating on trying to stabilise the patient, who was still howling in agony.

'Charlotte, call the plastic surgeon,' Jago instructed. 'He needs more pain relief so we'll give him an injection of calcium gluconate. And then we need to take some bloods. Fluoride ions are absorbed by the skin.'

'Even when it's only damaged a small surface area?' Katy gave the injection under the skin and then started to search for a vein.

'You can get problems with as little as a two per cent body surface area burn when the chemical is concentrated 70 per cent hydrofluoric acid. Fluoride ions end up in the circulation and produce a variety of systemic problems. We'll check his calcium and magnesium levels and his U and Es,' Jago told her, nodding approval as Charlotte appeared with a cardiac monitor. 'Good. We need to get him wired up so that we can keep an eye on his ECG.'

As Charlotte connected the machine to the patient, Katy watched the wavy line on the screen, seeing that it was showing a normal heart rate.

They waited for the results of the blood tests and in the meantime the plastic surgeon arrived to assess the burns.

'Hmm. Nasty.' He examined them closely and pulled a face. 'Some of those burns are full thickness. There's a bed on the ward so I'll admit him and take it from there.'

Jago gave a full handover and Charlotte arranged for the patient to be transferred to the ward.

'What will happen now?' Katy asked, after they were finally left on their own.

'Well, he's probably going to need skin grafts to at least some of those burns,' Jago said, finishing off the notes and sliding his pen back in his pocket. 'Now, on to more important matters. What are you cooking me for dinner?'

Katy worked through to the end of her shift and made her way home via the supermarket where she picked up some food for supper.

Realising that she'd never actually cooked a meal for Jago before, she felt a smile touch her lips. She was looking forward to it.

Chopping onion and garlic, she suddenly heard the sound of a key in the door.

Expecting to see Libby, she turned with a smile on her

face, excited at the prospect of confessing that she was going to marry Jago.

Her father stood in the hallway.

The smile on her face died. Katy felt her heart rate double and suddenly her palms were damp.

Reminding herself that she was twenty-nine years of age and that he couldn't touch her any more, she dropped the knife she was holding and tried to control her shaking legs.

'Dad! How did you get in?'

'I've got a key.'

Well, of course he had, Katy thought dully. Somehow, somewhere her father had managed to obtain a key to her flat. And now he was inside. And she was in trouble.

'Did you want something?'

He moved towards her, his powerful bulk blocking the doorway of the kitchen, his expression ugly. 'You're seeing Rodriguez again.'

Her heart lurched and she fought the impulse to take several steps backwards. 'That's none of your business.'

She didn't even question how he knew. Her father knew everything.

'I wondered why you made that nonsensical speech about breaking off your engagement,' he growled. 'I should have guessed it was Rodriguez. And don't try denying it. I had a call from a journalist today. They've got pictures of you together.'

Katy stared at him blankly. Pictures?

How?

They'd been in Spain, for goodness' sake. Who on earth had managed to take a picture of them?

'Some nonsense about you saving a life in Spain.' Her father gave a dismissive snort. 'It's everywhere. Take a tip from me—next time you want to run away with your boyfriend, be more discreet.'

'And leave someone lying by the roadside?' Katy looked at him with incredulity, registering just how callous he was.

'And for your information, I wasn't running away with anyone.'

'But you're seeing him. I can't believe you'd be stupid enough to see Rodriguez again. I thought I'd managed to get rid of him eleven years ago,' her father said nastily, taking another step into the room.

Suddenly realising that she could smell alcohol on his breath, she felt her stomach lurch with fear. 'I want you to leave,' she said quietly. 'We can talk about this another time.'

'There's nothing more to talk about.' He lifted a hand and stabbed a finger towards her. 'You're marrying Freddie, my girl, and that's the end of it.'

'I'm marrying Jago!'

The moment the impulsive declaration left her lips she knew she'd made a mistake and she closed her eyes briefly, cursing her stupidity.

Dear God, she never should have said that.

In his current mood, goodness only knew what her father was capable of.

He stared at her for a moment, stunned into silence by her passionate announcement, swaying slightly as he stood. 'You're marrying *Rodriguez*?'

Katy stood still, frozen to the spot, hardly daring to breathe.

Her father gave a short laugh. 'Then you're more of a fool than I thought you were. Do you really think he loves you?' He gave a derisive snort. 'Of course he doesn't. He's just using you. He wants your name, your reputation and your money. But most of all he wants revenge.'

Revenge?

She knew Jago wasn't interested in any of the first three things, but revenge? Was it possible that her father was right?

After all, she knew that Jago didn't love her.

Was that why he'd asked her to marry him? Because he knew that it would be the ultimate revenge on her father?

Filled with doubts, she suddenly wanted to be on her own.

She lifted her head and looked at her father. He'd done it again. Put doubts in her mind. Tried to ruin everything.

'Go away.' She couldn't keep the choke out of her voice. 'Just leave me alone. This is my life. *My life.*' She never raised her voice but she was shouting now, the frustration of years of dealing with her father's bully-boy tactics coming to a head. 'I don't ever want to see you again.'

Infuriated by her unusual attitude, her father stepped towards her.

'You'll marry Rodriguez over my dead body,' he roared, and then staggered as a powerful arm clamped itself like a vice around his throat and pulled him away from her.

Jago's tone was ice cold. 'If you ever lay a finger on Katy, that's exactly what's going to happen.'

Charles Westerling gave a grunt of anger and tried to free himself, but Jago powered him against the wall and held him easily, the muscles of his shoulders bunched as he used his strength to subdue the older man.

'When you agree to behave like a decent human being I'll let you go.' He spoke to Katy over his shoulder. '*Querida*, did he hurt you?'

Katy shook her head. 'No. Let him go, Jago. Please.'

She just wanted him out of the flat so that she could think.

Was Jago really just marrying her to get revenge?

As usual, her father had managed to destroy her fragile happiness with a few well-chosen words.

Jago frowned slightly and turned back to her father, his expression menacing. 'It is time we got a few things straight.' His voice was raw and angry and his Spanish accent was more pronounced than usual. 'I am marrying Katy with or without your approval. Your wishes are of absolutely no interest to us whatsoever. As you quite clearly cannot behave yourself you won't be invited to the wedding, and in future if you wish to see Katy you can only do so when I'm present.'

Her father gaped at him, stunned that anyone would dare to speak to him like that. 'You can't dictate when I see my daughter!'

'I just did.' Jago's eyes were as hard as flint. 'Understand that the first duty of a Spanish male is to protect the woman he loves. I repeat—you won't be seeing her unless I am present. Do you understand?'

Loves?

Katy heard the word and clung to it, desperate for any scrap of reassurance that came her way.

'That's outrageous.' Charles struggled against that vice-like grip but Jago refused to release him.

'No.' Jago's voice was ice cold. 'It's just the way it's going to be. Your chauffeur is outside. Better not keep him waiting.'

Her father staggered slightly as Jago released him and made a move to approach Katy, but Jago stepped in front of him, preventing access.

With a last furious grunt her father turned and strode out of the flat, past Libby who'd just returned from work.

Libby flinched as the door crashed shut and she shot Jago an apologetic look.

'It's a wonder we're even vaguely normal, isn't it?' she delivered calmly, dropping her bag on the floor and strolling into the kitchen. 'Always such a pleasure to have a visit from one's parents.'

Katy sank down on one of the kitchen chairs, her legs still shaking.

'He said that we're in the papers. Someone took a picture of us together when we stopped to help that girl.' She looked at Jago blankly. 'I didn't even notice anyone.'

'That's always the trouble with the paparazzi,' Libby

grumbled, reaching into the cupboard for a jar of peanut butter. 'If you don't notice them you can never give them your good side. Not that you have anything but a good side, it has to be said. I just hope you didn't damage my favourite shoes when you were performing heroics in the hot dust of Spain.'

Katy looked at her sister in exasperation and then laughed. Trust Libby to inject a bit of frivolity into the proceedings. 'Your shoes are back in your dressing room.'

'Phew. I can breathe again.' Libby smiled happily and started to eat peanut butter out of the jar with a spoon. 'I'm going to my room to watch something mindless. Night.'

Katy watched her go, aware that she hadn't even told Libby her news. All day she'd been bursting to tell her and then suddenly the bubble of excitement had burst. Thanks to her father.

Suddenly aware that Jago was watching her with an ominous frown, she stirred. 'I'm glad you arrived when you did,' she said quietly, and he tensed still further.

'Would he have hit you?' he demanded rawly. 'Has he ever hit you?'

Katy hesitated. 'Once,' she said finally. 'When I was a child.'

Jago's fists tightened, his fury unconcealed. 'What happened?'

'Alex hit him with a cricket bat,' Katy muttered, hating to remember those days. 'And Libby called the police.'

Jago threw back his head and laughed. 'You three do stick together, don't you?'

Katy nodded and gave a slight smile. 'He never, ever tried it again but he often came close, particularly when he drank too much. Which he did frequently.' She stared at her hands. 'The truth is that he found other, more clever methods of intimidating us.'

Jago frowned. 'Answer me something else...' He hesitated, running a hand over the back of his neck as he braced himself to ask the question. 'Was he the reason you lost the baby? Libby said that you fell.'

'It was my fault,' Katy said quickly. 'I wasn't looking where I was going and I fell down the stairs.'

Dark eyes locked onto hers with disturbing intensity. 'But why weren't you looking where you were going?'

She hesitated. 'Dad guessed I was pregnant,' she confessed quietly. 'He was shouting at me and…he scared me. I backed away and tripped. It was an accident.'

Jago looked at her in naked disbelief. 'You are so incredibly forgiving, *querida*. How can you bear to see him?'

'He's still my dad,' Katy said simply. 'And I've never given up hoping that one day he'll be proud of me. But I have to confess that these days we usually only get together for family gatherings. I would never choose to see him alone. He caught me by surprise, turning up here tonight. I didn't know he'd managed to get a key.'

'Well, that won't happen again,' Jago growled, stepping forward and pulling her into his arms. 'I'm staying with you tonight, and tomorrow you're moving in with me and I'll brief the security guards. He won't be allowed access.'

Katy stood unresisting in his arms, but the happiness that she'd felt since Spain had totally vanished.

Was Jago really marrying her to avenge himself on her father?

She'd never really understood his reasons for proposing. The only thing she knew for sure was that he didn't love her.

'Jago…' Her voice cracked. 'I—I've changed my mind about marrying you.'

How could she marry him when she knew he didn't love her and when there was so much unpleasant history between them? Her father had treated him appallingly. She could hardly blame him for wanting to extract the ultimate revenge, but that didn't mean that she wanted to be a part of it.

Jago was looking at her blankly. 'Sorry?'

She swallowed. 'I can't marry you, Jago.'

He tensed. 'If this is about Freddie—'

'It's nothing to do with Freddie. It just wouldn't work between us.'

There was a pulsing silence and when he finally spoke his tone was icy. 'This is about your father, isn't it? Did he say something?'

Tears stung her eyes. There was no point in telling him. He was bound to deny it even if it was the truth. She just had to face the fact that it could never work between them.

'It isn't about my father,' she lied. 'It's about us. I can't marry you.'

He stared at her for a long moment, those incredible dark eyes veiled so that she was totally unable to read his response.

Then he turned without another word and walked out of the door.

CHAPTER ELEVEN

KATY arrived at work feeling gritty-eyed from lack of sleep and too much crying.

The department was already in chaos with people standing in the waiting room and the corridors full of trolleys.

She dumped her bag in the staffroom and then found Charlotte. 'What on earth is going on here?'

'Don't ask me,' Charlotte muttered, sorting through a pile of notes and handing her a set. 'Can you start by seeing this guy for me? He's been waiting for four hours so he's bound to be in a good humour. Good luck.'

Relieved that no one had noticed that she'd been crying her heart out for most of the night, Katy made her way to one of the cubicles and used the intercom to call the patient through.

He was remarkably cheerful for someone who'd waited so long and she examined his injured ankle and sent him along for an X-ray.

'You couldn't weight bear after the accident, so we need to check it,' she told him, glancing up as Charlotte popped her head round the curtain, her face white.

'I need you in Resus.'

'On my way.' Katy stood up and gave her patient an apologetic smile. 'I'm so sorry. We're very busy today. Follow the red line to X-ray and then I'll see you when you come back.'

Wondering what was responsible for the tension she'd read in Charlotte's face, she made her way to Resus and stopped dead with shock when she saw her mother standing in the doorway.

'Mum? What are you doing here?'

Jago and Charlotte were already in action, and her eyes swivelled to the patient on the trolley who was being attached to a heart monitor.

'*Dad?*' Her voice was a croak and she felt a chill run through her body.

Jago's eyes collided with hers briefly and then he turned his attention back to her father as he put a line in and started an infusion. 'You don't have to be here, Katy,' he said roughly. 'Take your mother to the relatives' room.'

Her mother straightened her shoulders. 'I'm not leaving him,' she said stiffly, and Katy walked into the room, letting the door swing closed behind her.

She hurried up to the trolley, her brain working in slow motion. 'What happened?'

Her father was pale and sweaty, gasping for breath as he lay on the trolley.

'We were at home and he suddenly clutched his chest and complained of pains,' her mother said shakily, her eyes on Jago. 'I—I think another doctor should see him!'

'Mum!' Katy was aghast and she looked at Jago with mortification, but Jago didn't react, all his attention concentrated on her father.

'I'm fully aware that Mr Rodriguez hates your father,' her mother said dully, 'and I have to admit he has reason. Why would he want to help him?'

Intercepting Charlotte's startled glance, Katy slipped an arm round her mother. 'Jago's a brilliant doctor, Mum,' she said quietly. 'The best. Who Dad is, or what he's done, doesn't matter at the moment.'

There wasn't anyone else she'd want caring for a member of her family.

Feeling strangely disconnected, Katy watched as Jago examined her father, checking his peripheral pulses to exclude aortic dissection and checking his legs for any evidence of clots in the veins.

'Katy, either help me out here or get me another doctor,' Jago growled suddenly, and Katy leapt into action.

'What do you want me to do?' She wasn't capable of thinking straight but she could follow orders.

'Take blood for U and Es, glucose, CK, FBC, and we may as well check his cholesterol as well.' He glanced up. 'Charlotte, get him attached to a pulse oximeter. I want to monitor his oxygen saturation. And get a radiographer up here. I want a portable chest X-ray.'

'I've done an ECG trace.' Charlotte handed him the strip of paper and Jago ran it through his fingers, studying it carefully.

'He's got ST elevation and inverted T waves,' he said finally, interpreting what looked like a wavy line to the uninitiated.

But Katy knew that what he was describing were changes to the pattern of electrical activity in the heart.

'He's had an MI?'

Her mother glanced between them in confusion. 'What's an MI?'

'Myocardial infarction. It means that Dad's had a heart attack,' Katy explained gently, and Jago looked at her.

'What are his risk factors? Does he smoke? What's his blood pressure like normally?'

Katy opened her mouth but it was her mother who answered, her voice amazingly calm.

'He hasn't smoked for thirty years but his blood pressure has been worryingly high for months now and his GP has been warning him to slow down and take some exercise.'

Katy stared at her mother. It was the first she'd heard of it. *'Mum?'*

'You know your father—he never likes to show weakness,' her mother explained wearily. 'He's also had a very high cholesterol and I've had him on a strict diet. Unfortunately, I don't think he sticks to it when I'm not watching him.'

For the first time Katy realised just how much her mother must love her father. Maybe their marriage wasn't just a business arrangement after all.

She stood still, barely aware of the arrival of the radiographer who bustled around the room preparing to take the X-ray Jago had requested.

'Charlotte, call the coronary care team,' Jago ordered once the X-ray had been taken, adjusting the flow of oxygen through her father's mask. 'I've given him morphine for the pain and aspirin, and we've started thrombolytic therapy. He needs to be transferred to the unit.'

Charles gave a groan and Katy tiptoed to his side.

'It's all right, Dad,' she said quietly, aware that her mother was standing next to her, tears in her eyes.

'Do you hear that, Charles? Despite everything you've done, your daughter is prepared to offer you comfort. I hope you're ashamed of yourself.'

Katy blinked. 'Mum, this isn't the right time.'

'This is exactly the right time,' Caroline said calmly, her eyes fixed on her husband's face. 'If you want to apologise to Katy, then now would be a good time.'

Katy thought she must have misheard. She'd never heard her mother use that tone with her father before, and he was *ill*.

What was going on?

'Charles…' Her mother leaned forward and moved the oxygen mask slightly, her hand trembling. 'I know you can hear me. You know there's something that you want to say to your daughter.'

At that moment the doors to Resus swung open and Libby flew into the room, her blonde ponytail swinging wildly as she hurried across to them.

Aware that a family drama was unfolding, she stopped dead, glancing quizzically at Jago who shrugged his broad shoulders.

Charles opened his eyes and suddenly all the fight seemed to leave him.

'Come here, Katy.' He spoke with considerable difficulty and Jago frowned.

'He needs the oxygen, I don't think he should—'

His patient waved a hand feebly. 'I need to speak,' he said hoarsely, and Katy stepped closer, feeling her heart pounding. What was it that her father wanted to say?

'I haven't been…' He broke off and licked his lips. 'I owe you…'

Her mother's mouth tightened. 'Just say it, Charles!'

'What your mother means is that I'm sorry,' he croaked finally, closing his eyes and sinking against the back of the trolley which had been raised to allow him to be upright and thus improve his breathing. 'I didn't know just how much you loved Jago. I thought it was just a fling.'

Aware of Charlotte's round-eyed curiosity, Katy felt her face colour. The one time her father came near to an apology for his behaviour, it had to be in front of an audience.

And she didn't really want Jago reminded of how much she'd loved him.

Her father cleared his throat and fiddled with the mask. 'I thought you'd get over him, but you never did.'

'Dad, let's forget it now.' Mortified by the disclosure of such personal details, Katy wanted to fall through the floor.

'And he never got over you,' her father continued, turning his head with difficulty so that he could see Jago. 'When you told me that you loved her and wanted to marry her, I was furious. And worried. She was only eighteen and I thought you were wrong for her.'

Katy froze, wondering if her father was rambling. As a doctor she was well aware that a heart attack could cause confusion. Why else would he be saying that Jago loved her? Jago had never loved her. And he'd certainly never wanted to marry her.

'He's trying to apologise,' her mother said, 'but unfortunately he hasn't had much practice. I have to confess that it's probably my fault that he's had a heart attack. He came roaring back from your flat last night, told me what had happened and we had a blazing row.'

Katy stared.

They'd had a row?

To the best of her knowledge her mother had never answered her father back in the entire thirty-six years of their marriage.

Her father struggled to speak. 'I couldn't believe that you and Jago had found each other again and were planning to get married.'

'We're not.' Finally Jago intervened, his tone flat and emotionless. 'You can relax, Mr Westerling. You'll be relieved to hear that your daughter has refused to marry me.'

For some reason this seemed to agitate Charles, and Jago frowned. 'I think that's enough talk now. You need to relax. Everything can be sorted out later.'

Charles ignored him, gulping in air and staring at his daughter. 'I shouldn't have said it. Any of it. None of it was true. He loves you and he always did. And you love him. I suppose that's all that matters.'

Jago's eyes rested on Katy and his firm mouth tightened ominously.

'He said something to you?' His voice was soft. 'I should have guessed. What did he say to you, Katy? What was I supposed to have done?'

She licked dry lips, no longer caring that they had an audience. 'Revenge. He said that you only wanted to marry me because that would be the ultimate revenge.'

There was a long silence. 'And you believed him?'

'I couldn't think of any other reason you'd be marrying me.'

Jago inhaled deeply. 'Could you not?'

He looked at her thoughtfully, but before he could speak

the cardiologist arrived with his team and the attention turned back to her father.

Katy stood next to her father, feeling totally numb as Jago talked quietly to his colleague, explaining the history and discussing the ECG trace while the rest of the team listened.

She was only half-aware of what was going on as they examined her father again and made arrangements to transfer him to Coronary Care.

Satisfied that the cardiologists now had the situation well in hand, Jago strode over to the trolley.

'They're going to take you to Coronary Care now, Mr Westerling.' His gaze rested on the older man's face for a moment, his expression totally inscrutable, and Caroline sighed, indicating that she was completely aware of his conflicting emotions.

'Jago, we owe you so much. How can we ever thank you for what you've done? And how can we ever make amends for keeping the two of you apart for so long?'

Galvanised into action by those words, Jago wrenched off his gloves and tossed them into the bin. 'I don't care about that. All I care about at the moment is having a conversation with Katy without an audience.' He lifted his eyes to hers. 'In my office. Now.'

'I'll sort out the transfer,' Charlotte muttered, and Libby smiled weakly.

'Exciting, isn't it? Life with my family. I bet you can't wait for the next episode.' But her eyes were worried as they rested on her father and she stepped closer to the trolley.

Katy stood in Jago's office waiting for him, her legs trembling.

The door clicked shut and she turned on him, her voice shaking with passion. 'Eleven years ago did you really tell my father you wanted to marry me?'

He tensed, obviously surprised by the directness of her approach. 'Yes.'

She gave a groan and sank onto the chair as all the pieces of the jigsaw fell into place.

'So *that's* why my father was so determined to break us up. I could never understand why he was so worried that it was serious. You never seemed serious to me. You kept telling me that you didn't do commitment.'

'I didn't until I met you. When I saw you that day you fell off your horse, it took every ounce of willpower at my disposal not to roll you on your back in the grass and follow my baser instincts,' he confessed rawly, dragging his gaze away from her and pacing across the room to stare out of the window. 'You were so unlike the women I usually dated that I told myself that I had to back off.'

'I was so in love with you,' Katy muttered, 'but I never for one moment thought that you loved me, too. You showed absolutely no signs of it.'

He gave a groan and raked his fingers through his glossy dark hair. 'Of course I did, but you were just too inexperienced to see it. And I was afraid that what you were feeling for me was no more than a childish crush because I was your first lover.'

'My only lover, Jago,' she said quietly, and he stilled, every muscle in his powerful body suddenly tense as he absorbed what she'd just said.

'That can't be true.'

'After what I shared with you, I just couldn't bring myself to sleep with anyone else,' she confessed. 'I had several boyfriends, but when it came to it I just couldn't do it. Part of me always felt that I was yours.'

Jago was across the room in three long strides. 'Freddie?'

She shook her head. 'We were only ever friends. It was very much a marriage of convenience. He didn't even seem to mind when I ended it.'

A smile of pure male satisfaction suddenly transformed

his handsome face. 'He never knew the real you. Only I know how hot you can be.'

'Only when I'm with you.' She lifted her flushed face to his. 'I never, ever would have slept with another man, Jago.'

He groaned and dragged her to her feet, wrapping her in his arms. 'And I should never have even thought that of you. Have you any idea how bad I felt that day when you told me what your father had done? I can't believe I didn't see through it, but I was so blindly jealous at seeing you entwined with another man that I ceased to be capable of rational behaviour. And I can't believe that I left you pregnant. I'm so, so sorry about the baby, *querida*. Can you forgive me?'

'There's nothing to forgive,' she said, hugging him back. 'The baby wasn't your fault, and as for the rest of it…' She sighed and gave a slight shrug of her shoulders. 'I should have known that it was my father.'

'And I should have seen what he was doing,' he admitted ruefully, 'but it was only because I was so crazily in love with you and I'd never felt like that about anyone before. It clouded my judgement.'

Katy looked up at him, wobbly with love. 'That's what Libby said when I told her.'

'Well, your sister has more insight than either of us,' Jago groaned, running lean fingers through her silky hair with deep appreciation. 'Why do you think I kept those photographs? Looking at them caused me agony, but they were the only link I had with you. When I realised how badly I'd treated you I just didn't know what to do. I didn't know how to make you love me again.'

'I always loved you,' Katy said simply, lifting a finger to touch his rough jaw. 'Always. I never stopped loving you.'

He froze to the spot, obviously not daring to believe what he was hearing. 'You still love me?'

'So much that it terrifies me,' she confessed shakily, and he gave a disbelieving laugh.

'I can't believe I can be that lucky,' he said hoarsely, 'or that your father nearly ruined it again by making you believe that I was only marrying you out of revenge.'

'I couldn't see any other reason.' She coloured slightly. 'You hadn't thought to mention that you were in love with me.'

He groaned and dragged her against him. 'I thought it was obvious from the way we were together in Spain.'

'Not to me,' she said simply, and he stroked her hair away from her face with his free hand.

'I was working so hard at getting back into your good books that I didn't know what to do. I thought that even if I did tell you that I loved you, you were unlikely to believe me.' He gave a wry smile. 'And I have to admit that I've never been very good with the emotional stuff.'

'That's not true.' She wasn't letting him off the hook that easily. 'I've seen you with relatives, Jago, and I remember how you were with me at eighteen. I *know* you have a sensitive side.'

He gave a reluctant grin that turned her heart upside down. 'Just don't tell anyone. Not that I'll have any credibility left once Charlotte starts talking.' His smile faded and he looked down into her eyes. 'I have never stopped loving you, *querida*. But I thought that you had stopped loving me, and proud Spaniards are not the best at putting their hearts on the line.'

Stunned by his frank confession, she stood on tiptoe and kissed him. 'I think we better have a rule that once a day we tell each other absolutely everything that we're feeling, no matter how uncomfortable.'

He lowered his head with a groan and returned the kiss. 'I think you might be right. So, does this mean that you will marry me after all?'

She gave a shy nod and his grip tightened.

'I'm tempted to call the hospital chaplain and see if he can do it now, before your father comes up with any more of his inventive plans to keep us apart.'

She gave a shaky laugh and bit her lip. 'I can't believe that he said all that. Mum must have given him a real talking to, and she's *never* done that before.'

'Women can be scary when they're crossed,' Jago said, a hint of amusement in his deep drawl. 'I should know. I'll never forget your reaction when I told you about those photographs. I thought you were going to lynch me for being so stupid. And to think I once believed you were shy and gentle.'

She tipped her head on one side. 'I've changed.'

'But, thankfully, not that much, *querida*,' he murmured, kissing her until her head started to swim. 'You still love me.'

Katy clutched at his shirt for support. 'With all my heart.'

And registering the tenderness in his eyes, this time she just *knew* that nothing would ever come between them again. They belonged together for the rest of their lives.

A month later Libby helped put the finishing touches to Katy's wedding dress at the doorway of the church.

'You look spectacular,' she sighed, 'and I just *love* the shoes.'

Katy stared doubtfully at her feet. 'I don't know why I let you talk me into them. I feel as though I'm on stilts. I'm going to trip, going down the aisle.'

'You'll be holding Dad's arm,' Libby pointed out, sitting back on her heels and pulling a face. 'Who would have thought it? Dad suddenly having an entire personality change. It's as if that heart attack made him rethink his whole life.'

'And Mum seems so happy,' Katy agreed.

'Who knows? One day we might be a normal family,'

Libby quipped, straightening the hem of Katy's dress. 'OK, you're done. Go wow them.'

Katy looked down at herself. 'Do the shoes make me too tall?'

'You look stunning,' Libby said dryly. 'Fortunately, you're marrying a man who dwarfs you, so you don't need to spend the rest of your life wearing flats.'

Katy felt her stomach tumble at the thought of Jago waiting for her inside the church, with Alex as best man. 'I love him *so* much.'

'I know.' Libby scrambled to her feet and grinned. 'You always did.'

'I almost married Freddie.'

Libby shook her head. 'I hate to break this to you, but that was never going to happen. Alex and I would have kidnapped you rather than let you make a mistake like that.'

'I'm going to miss living with you so much.' Katy leaned forward and hugged her tightly. 'Alex is lucky to be moving in with you. I know you'll get on well.'

She said it very firmly, as if she was trying to convince herself, and Libby laughed.

'You know we'll probably kill each other,' she said dryly, and Katy sighed.

'Well, hopefully it won't be for long,' she said wistfully. 'I want you to meet someone and settle down.'

'Me?' Libby looked startled. 'You've got to be kidding. I'm a born-again cynic. Now, get down that aisle and stop fantasising.'

At that moment their father appeared, looking remarkably good considering his recent illness.

'The minute we've walked down that aisle you have to sit down,' Katy reminded him firmly, and he looked at her with eyes that were unusually bright.

'I've told everyone that my daughter is a doctor,' he said gruffly, taking her hand in his and tucking it into his arm.

'I know I've never said that I'm proud of you, but I am. Very proud. And I'm proud of you, too, Elizabeth.'

Aware that Libby's mouth had fallen so wide open that she was in danger of swallowing a large insect, Katy couldn't hide her smile.

'Thanks, Dad.' Apparently almost meeting his maker and a confrontation with his wife had been sufficient to make Charles seriously reconsider his ways.

As she heard the music start she moved to the top of the aisle and caught her first glimpse of Jago, standing tall and broad-shouldered next to her brother.

At that moment he turned and saw her and there was no missing the love and pride in his dark eyes. And as Katy took her first steps towards him on her father's arm, she knew that everything about her life was perfect.

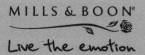

MILLS & BOON®

Live the emotion

Medical Romance™

DOCTOR AT RISK by Alison Roberts

Dr Ross Turnball and Nurse Wendy Watson fell in love on an Urban Search and Rescue course. It ended explosively, with a dramatic mission to rescue people from a bombed shopping mall – and an accident that nearly claimed Ross's life. Now he is struggling to regain his health, and is terrified he'll lose Wendy's love…

THE DOCTOR'S OUTBACK BABY
by Carol Marinelli

When a new and very English doctor, Timothy Morgan, arrives at Tennengarrah Clinic, Nurse Clara Watts finds her life running out of control. In the scorching heat of the Outback Clara and Tim are thrown together and whilst treating patients, find themselves hurtling towards an exciting affair.

THE GREEK CHILDREN'S DOCTOR
by Sarah Morgan

Libby Westerling has put herself up for sale at a charity auction to raise funds for the children's ward she works on. Libby is not in the market for a man – in fact, she's asked her brother to buy her! But instead, cool, sexy Dr Andreas Christakos makes the highest bid! How can she possibly work with him now?

On sale 2nd April 2004

Available at most branches of WHSmith, Tesco, Martins, Borders, Eason, Sainsbury's and all good paperback bookshops.

0304/03a

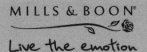

FREE

4 BOOKS
AND A SURPRISE GIFT!

We would like to take this opportunity to thank you for reading this Mills & Boon® book by offering you the chance to take FOUR more specially selected titles from the Medical Romance™ series absolutely FREE! We're also making this offer to introduce you to the benefits of the Reader Service™—

★ FREE home delivery   ★ FREE gifts and competitions
★ FREE monthly Newsletter   ★ Exclusive Reader Service discount
★ Books available before they're in the shops

Accepting these FREE books and gift places you under no obligation to buy; you may cancel at any time, even after receiving your free shipment. Simply complete your details below and return the entire page to the address below. ***You don't even need a stamp!***

YES! Please send me 4 free Medical Romance books and a surprise gift. I understand that unless you hear from me, I will receive 6 superb new titles every month for just £2.69 each, postage and packing free. I am under no obligation to purchase any books and may cancel my subscription at any time. The free books and gift will be mine to keep in any case.

M4ZEF

Ms/Mrs/Miss/Mr ....Initials ....
BLOCK CAPITALS PLEASE

Surname ....

Address ....

....

....Postcode ....

Send this whole page to:
UK: FREEPOST CN81, Croydon, CR9 3WZ
EIRE: PO Box 4546, Kilcock, County Kildare (stamp required)